HOW THE WORLD ENDS

BOOK
ONE

RUDOLF
KERKHOVEN

Product Artwork by Whitney Siemens

ALSO BY RUDOLF KERKHOVEN

The Year We Finally Solved Everything
A Dream Apart
Love is not free. The price is 99 cents.
How the World Ends (Book Two) (2018)
How the World Ends (Book Three) (2018)

ALSO BY RUDOLF KERKHOVEN & DANIEL PITTS

The Adventures of Whatley Tupper
The Redemption of Mr. Sturlubok
The Most Boring Book Ever Written
Can Stuart Henry Zhang Save the World?

IF YOU LIKE THIS NOVEL, PLEASE REVIEW IT
AT AMAZON.COM. IT HELPS.

.

CONTENTS

THE
BEGINNING

Alex slipped, landing on his knees and sliding down with both hands outstretched against the soil that rolled beneath his fingertips, a conveyor that he could not grab hold of. His father reached down to catch him but the boy gripped onto a hunched, protruding root and came to a halt. "Are you alright?" the man asked with wide iceberg eyes, curls of black hair dangling from either side of his cavernous cheeks. He was short of breath, face flushed, not by exertion but instead from the thought of his son's tumbling and irreversible descent: how a single, fumbled misstep could so callously erase all the life that came before it.

"I'm okay," Alex said, conscious of his father's expression. "I'm okay."

"You have to watch your step. This is a mountain. It deserves your respect."

Alex nodded and mumbled a vague acknowledgement while regaining his footing. He pretended to understand the meaning of the word, *respect*. He knew it was important, something that adults used to demonstrate their virtuousness, to show that they were kind individuals. He understood its essence when instructed to respect his Dad, to respect his elders. But when Alex's father told him to respect a tree and its fruit, told him to respect a goat before it was slaughtered, told him to respect those insects that survive the most profound of life's calamities—*told him to respect a mountain*—then Alex knew to nod, to feign acceptance.

His father grabbed onto a dangling cedar branch and pulled himself up the exposed rock to avoid placing weight onto his bad foot. Every other step was abbreviated and yet he remained confident on this steep incline. "Come on," he said, holding out one hand to clasp.

"I said, I'm okay." Alex replied, scampering up on all fours. "Is it much farther?"

His father nodded.

Alex sighed, keeping both eyes on the withered, copper needles beneath his feet.

"Trust me. It's going to be amazing. It's like nothing else you've ever seen"

"I know. I know."

Alex thought he knew. He called it *The Beanstalk* even though he was fully aware that it wasn't a plant and had nothing to do with the fairy tale. He'd analyzed pencil-sketched drawings on wrinkled white paper. He'd overheard the words of adults that described this enormous structure with vocabulary and allusions that did not make sense to a six-year-old boy. His father assured him that he needed to see it with his own eyes to appreciate its "profound scale." And again, Alex's thoughts would return to the copy of that picture book still occupying a sliver of their living room bookshelf, yellowing lines of tape adhering the many tears that traced the spine and dog-eared corners on almost every page.

"So, what is it?" Alex asked, searching through the trunks of trees in hope of catching a glimpse of its *profound scale*. All he could see were other mountains. The entire world was an endless series of wrinkled peaks.

"I don't know," his father said, trying to mask his annoyance, not with the question, but with the fact that this had all been discussed numerous times before.

"But it's not really a beanstalk?"

"It's not really a beanstalk."

"And they made it?"

"They made it."

"When did they make it?"

"Before you were born."

"On the Fourteenth of August?"

"Sometime after that."

"And what does it do?"

His father forced another sigh into a chuckle. "You know that I don't know."

"How come I can't see it if it's so big?"

"Because it's so far away."

"Farther away than those mountains?"

"Yes. A lot farther away than those mountains."

"I'm hungry."

"I know."

"Can we stop and have a snack?"

"Soon."

"How soon?"

"Soon."

"We must be close?"

His father didn't answer. This was the third time in as many months that they'd attempted the ascent, each of the previous journeys concluding with Alex being carried down on his father's back before reaching the peak. Alex had lived his entire life surrounded by mountains and yet he clearly couldn't appreciate their size, their *profound scale,* how he could hike for hours and still be told that there was so much left to climb. Perhaps that was what it meant to respect a mountain, he thought: they are big.

Although pleased that he was able to take a rest and eat as many dried blueberries and slices of jerky as he wished, Alex knew what this implied. They were still a long way off. They'd been hiking since the first light of dawn, leaving their home long before the blue sky of day smothered the last of the swirling, luminous nightlights. Alex was excited when he awoke; he could hardly sleep the night before. His father really believed that he was ready to make it this time. It just wasn't fair that the trek took so long. Looking up the mountainside, the arching ferns and wrinkly trunks never seemed to extend much farther. They had to be close, he'd think. And yet they weren't. Every time they'd come across another pink plastic ribbon tied tight around the stalk of a lanky birch, Alex hoped that this would signal that the end was near. But there was always another, barely visible, a pastel spec in this murky undergrowth. He wanted to admit to his father how weary his legs had become, but it was too late to turn back. His dad would tell him that it didn't matter, that he could do it, that he had to respect this mountain, or something.

Alex stood up, nodding with exaggerated swings of his chin to his father's reminders of being careful, and grabbed a stick from the ground, his eyes drawn to its smooth bark and a clean, snake-tongue split at one end. "Would this have made a good marshmallow stick?"

The man laughed, caught by surprise, "That would have made a perfect marshmallow stick."

Alex turned back, holding it in the air above an imaginary fire, fascinated by the idea of a marshmallow. There were so many things that adults reminisced about which made no sense to Alex, which he had no intention of understanding. But marshmallows! As light as a mushroom and yet composed of just sugar. Held above a flame, and the snow-white exterior would inflate to a crackling, golden brown. It was magic. Edible magic. Without looking back towards his father, Alex said: "We should try making marshmallows again."

"I don't think it would work out like you'd want."

"But can we try again? Please?"

"What you're going to see is way cooler than a marshmallow. Trust me."

Alex nodded, not because he agreed with his father but because he knew that it would appease him. He banged the stick against a rock, looking out towards the distant peaks, recognizing only Skihist Mountian and hopeful that his father wouldn't quiz him on the names of any others.

A glistening black slug rested motionless on a bed of bloodshot needles. Alex knelt closer, now able to trace its glistening, meandering path that originated from the swollen roots of a cedar. A pair of antennae searched, two fingers feeling around in the dark, oblivious to the hominid that towered above, staring down. As Alex shuffled another step closer, the creature withdrew its protuberances and shriveled in defense. He poked it with his stick and the mollusk compressed into a dense mound. It could have been a fallen nut or a wrinkled, decomposing leaf. Prodding it further, the slug resisted Alex's attempts to roll it over.

"What are you doing?" his father asked. "Just leave it alone."

Alex sighed. He wanted to step on it. He thought he still might.

"It's not hurting you. Come on, now. Let's go before it gets too hot."

The boy stared at the immobile creature, knocked it one last time, and turned to follow.

There it was. His father had limped ahead with excited steps and called out, "You can see it," his voice breathless, his arm extended and pointing through the thinning trunks of trees. It didn't look like a beanstalk. No matter what Alex had been told, he still visualized something green, a snaking weave of leafy vines that would extend into the shroud of clouds that capped the sky. Alex stopped climbing, grabbed onto his father's outstretched hand without looking. It didn't make sense. It was too distant for details, to have any discernable color. And yet it could not be missed: a great vertical shadow, snaking like a gnarled branch held upright into the sky where it radiated auburn against the hazy ceiling of the atmosphere and out into the cold dead of space. It made any one of these mountains that he'd spent the entire morning scampering up appear like a lone fern beneath a looming, ancient fir. Nothing could be so massive. Alex winced and rubbed his eyes as if it was a mistake. The entire southern sky was cracked.

"What is it?"

"I said, I don't know."

"Are there giants up there?"

His father chuckled. "It's not a beanstalk, remember?"

"What is it?"

"I don't know."

Alex kept squeezing his father's hand. "I'm scared."

"It's okay to be scared."

"Are you scared?"

"I was."

"You're not scared anymore?"

"I don't think so."

"You don't think so?"

"I'm not scared."

"Why not?"

"Because I think we're safe."

"You think we're safe?"

The man squeezed Alex's hand and looked him in the eyes with a tender smile intended to make his forthcoming lie appear as genuine as possible. The same comforting, essential falsehood that his own parents had repeated to him, assured him, on countless occasions before their deaths.

"Trust me. We're going to be fine."

PART
ONE

On a clear but muggy day in August of 2007, without effort and without awareness, Alex Maclean sliced through her left index finger with the piercing tip of a sturdy and inflexible chef's knife. Sara was just across the hall pretending to nap. Caleb was in the basement pretending to practice the piano. The compact disc that Alex had been listening to came to its conclusion but she hadn't noticed. She listened to the sequential patter of those same four keys that Caleb cycled through. The timing was off, his ring finger just a little too eager to pluck. Alex could visualize him leaning with his left elbow at the lip of the piano, his head resting in his palm. His eyes were probably closed, she thought, while his right hand tapped the keys like bored fingers against a desk. Alex didn't know how to play. All she knew was that the black keys sounded "off" and the white keys were "on." Two years of lessons and this was all that Caleb could perform: four notes in an infinite and ill-timed loop. She wanted to tell him to stop. To practice whatever it was that Ms.

Chen had intended. Three thousand dollars for a piano deserved more than this. But Alex didn't budge, unaware of the blood running down her finger, over the cutting board, pooling about the julienned red peppers. She looked out over the sink and through the window towards the back fence. Caleb stopped. Her house was quiet. There was nothing to see. Blood dribbled over the edge of the scuffed wooden board and onto the speckled black granite countertop. Alex felt like an iron shaving quivering at the hazy edge of a magnetic field, the moment it trembles before hurtling inwards without control. She stared out the window and heard something drip. A leaky faucet. The eaves after a rainfall. She glanced down to her feet and saw a splattered pool of blood against the amber hardwood. She never wanted to keep those worn fir boards in the kitchen, even if they were almost a hundred years old, even if it gave their house the cachet of coolness that couldn't be found in a modern build. Blood was trickling down between her bare feet from the counter above. She followed the trail upwards, a camera panning for dramatic effect, inspecting the narrow stream along the counter top, the cardinal puddle on the cutting board, a gleaming chef's knife, and that deep, linear gouge within an index finger. The ridged edges of skin had parted, revealing layers of milky tissue and dark violet gelatin. The finger twitched with each throbbing beat of her heart.

This was her finger.

As if the magnet had been withdrawn and the iron shaving tumbled back into place, Alex realized that she was staring at her own hand. This was her own blood. She gasped a scream, already out of breath, and stumbled into the island behind her. There was blood everywhere. It was running down her finger and onto her tights. Caleb resumed playing the piano. She thought of yelling for help. She wanted to tell him to stop. She stepped forward and swatted the tap to unleash a torrent of cold water. Inching her finger closer, the stream pried apart her wound and a wave of nausea sprinted up from her stomach. "Caleb," she called out, her breaths light. "Caleb," she repeated.

He was then standing above her as she tried to focus on the ceiling, his beautiful eyes wide, fearful that his mother was dying.

Alex waited for Hayden to make a joke about it. She expected him to do so not because he'd conclude that it would be prudent to lighten the mood, but because he refused to accept the significance of his wife's concerns. Alex wondered if Hayden took anything she did or thought seriously, be it her worries, her interests, her desires. He asked why there were bandages on her finger and she told him that she'd cut herself while preparing dinner—but there was more, she strained to impress upon him. She didn't remember the act. For a moment, she was disconnected. When she noticed the blood, she just observed, not feeling a thing. It was like something inside her came unplugged for a few moments. There was that sensation. "An iron shaving being enveloped by a magnetic force," were her words. She thought they were apt. She'd spent that afternoon searching for an appropriate analogy.

Hayden didn't even nod. He looked at his phone and nodded (he never used to be the type of person to incessantly check for messages and updates, but this was not just any phone, this was an *i*Phone, *the* definite article of modernity and innovation; now his eyes were sure to droop downwards to the palm of his hand several times a minute). She inspected his face, those long lines that traced the borders of each cheek, like finger marks in wet sand, and the quivering, clenching movements of his black eyebrows. In the fifteen years that they'd been together, it was only his eyes—a sunburst of silver that radiated out into a tanzanite blue—that never aged or changed. She could still get lost in them, taken back to when his hair was long, a uniform black that framed his expression like curtains pulled aside a stage. Now those eyes wouldn't look at her, hidden behind the swooping curls of premature gray that hung past the ridged lines of his forehead. He was more interested in his iPhone than the fact that his wife should have acquired sutures for her wound. He walked past her and went to the washroom. So that he could spend more time on his phone.

At dinner, Alex was sure that Hayden would finally mutter some comment in jest. He'd agreed to keep his phone away at mealtimes—mostly because it was too great a temptation for Caleb—and some "humor" would be his way of passing the time. Back when Caleb was still an infant, both agreed that there would be no more dinners in front of the television. They would sit together as a family and eat, a prerequisite to a healthy household. And for nine years they kept it up, sitting together, waiting for the last person to take a seat, demanding that Caleb asked to be excused before exiting. This evening—on that clear but muggy day in August of 2007—there was nothing being said. Alex could hear Caleb chew with his mouth open. She wanted to tell him to keep his lips together. Sara stabbed a stalk of asparagus with a fork and then grabbed a carrot with her fingers. Hayden looked up to Alex and smirked.

Here it comes, she thought.

"You know," He put down his fork and looked towards his wife. "I didn't realize you thought that we weren't getting enough iron in our diets. Personally, I'd rather just eat spinach."

Alex nodded with a grimace.

He laughed as if someone else had delivered the punchline. "You know, you didn't have to cut yourself to—"

"I get it."

He required a few more seconds to let loose those last chucking gasps. It was that amusing.

Caleb looked between his mother and father. "What's funny?"

Alex answered: "Nothing."

"It was pretty funny."

"Then how come I'm not laughing?"

Hayden shrugged, his cheeks still dimpled from a grin. "I don't know. Too soon, I guess."

Alex shook her head.

"I'm sorry. I'm sorry," Hayden held up his hands, which she knew was his attempt to diffuse the situation but only pissed her off further by implying that she was an irritable and combustive bitch in contrast to his easy-going and diplomatic composure. After all, he was the first to throw up the white flag. But Alex knew that it was bullshit. Should something be a joke to Hayden, then it was a given that everyone else should find the topic equally trivial. But if Hayden was in a cantankerous mood, then one better not say a word, for there were pressing matters at hand. He was no longer Hayden but instead Dr. Maclean—and the good doctor had matters of pivotal importance on his mind. He would remove himself from the distractions of his family and sequester himself in his attic office or, much more likely, at the university. A location where real work was accomplished. Because this, right here, at the family home, was a place where only trifling events occurred. Matters of personal and familial importance, but nothing more. Nothing in that *big scheme of things*.

"Hey," Hayden said, his expression now morose while intending to be conciliatory. "I thought it would lighten the mood, but I guess it was too soon. I'm sorry."

Alex didn't have a choice. Sara and Caleb were at the table. She had to assure him that no apologies were necessary and then move on. That was Hayden's masterstroke, right there: he waited until the family dinner, that sacred Maclean family tradition, for him to make his stupid joke. She could not retaliate. She could not impress upon him that what happened was not just an accident. For a moment, she was removed from herself. For a moment, she wasn't herself, she wasn't anyone. She just stood there and witnessed her finger and the tissue underneath. She watched as the digit twitched like a broken second-hand. She just watched. This was not normal. This was not something that *just happens from time to time*. This was a sign of someone losing her mind.

Housewife. What a horrid word, Alex thought. It implied marriage not so much to a husband but to the house, to the cleaning, to the cooking, to the errands, to arranging the knick-knacks, to having polite conversation with the neighbors, to dealing with temperamental toddlers, to chatting with the school teacher, to unwinding knotted car-seat straps, to making sure everything was *just* right for when the husband returns home from work—work that requires years of post-secondary training, work that dictates the lives of other adults, work that offers growing sums of money as compensation. And it wasn't just a matter of semantics. Alex didn't want to be a stay-at-home-mother. This wasn't the plan when they first spoke of having children. This wasn't the plan when she had Caleb. But, "*it just makes sense*," Hayden started saying. Opposition to the idea implied being irrational at best and selfish at worst. *It just makes sense.*

Alex used to do work that required years of post-secondary training, work that dictated the lives of other adults, work that offered growing sums of money in compensation. For most of their time together, Alex earned far more than Hayden. She managed teams in post-production visual effects, her (maiden) name in the credits of motion pictures that grossed over a billion dollars worldwide. It was her job to keep teams of disparate personalities—aimless artists, introverted computer engineers and alpha (fe)male producers—cohesive and productive. She didn't liken herself to being some *essential piece of the puzzle,* but instead she was the person who put that puzzle together. Without Alex, no matter the skills and creative genius of these people, they were scattered pieces within a box. She was the one who positioned everything together, the undulating teeth and grooves of each individual, the contrasting personalities and desires of dozens of colleagues. For more than a decade, Alex was in a profession that demanded respect and admiration. And more than anything else, when people learned what Alex did, they said the same word: "Cool." And they meant it.

No one replies that way upon being informed that you are a housewife.

But the entire motion-picture post-production industry is one of contract work. You are hired for a project. And then you move on to another project. There will always be movies, yes, but there will also always be another company willing to offer the same services faster, cheaper, and maybe even better.

Before Caleb, losing her job didn't matter. She would find another. If not immediately, then she and Hayden would travel. After all, he was the perpetual graduate student; his schedule was not so much flexible as it was nebulous, and a near limitless pool of student loans could always be drawn upon with mere clicks of a mouse. After Caleb was born, she took a year off and then went back to work part-time. In those hectic weeks before a production deadline, Hayden would stay home. *It just made sense.* Then Hayden graduated with his Ph.D. in economics. Then Hayden was offered a tenure-track position at Simon Fraser University, in the inner suburbs of Vancouver. Then Hayden started his own consultation business. Then Hayden had predictable and growing income. When Sara arrived (four years and one miscarriage later than planned) and Alex was once again on the precipice of a concluding contract, it just made sense for her to stay home indefinitely. No need to pay exorbitant sums for daycare. No need for both adults to spend their weeks sprinting from one obligation to another without ever having time to relax with their children. They could afford Alex staying home. Hayden's consulting company was getting work from outside the city and country (although Alex found it ironic how with her, it was contract work; with Hayden, it was consulting). He would need to travel more often, but he could afford his family having a comfortable life without Alex dealing with the fickle and frugal digital effects industry. "It just makes sense," Hayden said, not even twenty weeks into her pregnancy with Sara. And Alex agreed—it made sense for Sara to stay home with her mother instead of going to daycare; it made sense for Caleb to get picked up and dropped off at school instead of going to some before-and-after center; and it *really* made sense for Hayden, for he could fly to any conference in any metropolis confident that his dutiful housewife was keeping everything together for him. Alex just wasn't convinced that it made sense for her. But there she was again, being selfish.

Sara and Caleb were asleep. Hayden was upstairs in his office. Alex sat on the living room sofa with the late evening news on in the background, a nightly routine passed down from her dead father. The wooden floor between Hayden and herself was far too aged and shallow to muffle even the slightest movements and yet Alex hadn't heard a sound from her husband in half an hour. She could imagine his blank expression as he stared at the laptop display, his eyes rolling past updated NHL statistics. Important work to be done. Normally, Alex would have a glass of wine at this point—another routine passed down from her dead father, although one she adhered to with far less enthusiasm—but she wanted to remain entirely sober this evening. Maybe she'd been drinking too much over these last years? Maybe that was why her brain switched off in the middle of the day while slicing red peppers? It was impossible for her to avoid that same thought: maybe this was what happened when her father first started to lose his wit, his memories, his personality. Maybe it started with these skips in his cognizance, like a needle on an old vinyl record. Alex once again ran her fingers over the bandages, squeezing just enough to elicit discomfort but not pain.

There was a story from China on the television. The entire populace of a village was found drowned in a nearby river. While impossible to determine the details, there was no doubt that at least two hundred people had perished. The correspondent relayed vague rumors of an industrial accident and subsequent cover-up. But this couldn't answer how *everyone* in the town would fall into the river. Chinese officials were denying the most nefarious claims but remained unable to offer their own explanation. The accompanying clunky and pixelated video showed empty buildings and narrow, gravel streets under the bright light of day before switching to limp, sodden corpses being aligned in rows along a muddy riverbank. The report was a minute in length, a minor story broadcast to acknowledge the burbling social media interest about this incident. But in the end, there was nothing to report aside from "something strange happened in a village in China." The anchor then alluded to some great weather continuing on in the forecast before going into a commercial break.

When Hayden came to bed, he expected Alex to be asleep. He slid beside her, back inches from her own.

Alex rolled over, "Did you read about that village in China?"

"You weren't sleeping?"

"I couldn't sleep."

"You've just been lying there?"

"Maybe I slept for a little. I don't know. I don't think so. But did you hear about that village in China?"

"What village in China?"

"Then I guess you didn't hear about it."

Hayden sighed, presumably exhausted after working with such diligence for the last few hours. "What happened?"

Alex felt no pity. She knew that he'd spent at least half of his time looking at sports highlights. "This whole village jumped into a river. Everyone. They were found upstream."

Hayden shrugged. This story lacked much of a plot. "Probably a cover-up for something?"

"What could make an entire village drown?"

"Is this what you've been thinking about while you've been lying in bed?"

Alex didn't reply.

Hayden said, "You should get more sleep."

"I'm not lying here thinking about this because I want to. It's just what I'm thinking about."

Hayden didn't reply. He kissed Alex just at the nape of her neck and rolled over. "Well, I'm tired. I'm sure I'll read about it tomorrow." Alex looked towards the drawn horizontal blinds, feeling the nudging throb of her left index finger with each heartbeat. She closed her eyes, wishing that Hayden would kiss her in that spot just one more time. She couldn't ask him. If she solicited this then it wouldn't tingle like before. Hayden didn't move. Alex imagined a family—mother, father, nine-year-old son and three-year-old daughter—sprinting towards a riverbank. The adults have a look of furious intent. The son follows obediently. And the daughter is held in her mother's arms, oblivious to their fate. First the father leaps in, then his son, and finally the mother and daughter. They plummet into the milky brown water with hardly a ripple. No one tries to swim. They descend to the bottom like rocks.

Alex could find no mention of the Chinese village in any of the news. What little she found through a Google query brought up nothing more detailed than what she'd seen the night before. She watched the midday news, then the evening news, keeping the television on in the background throughout the day. There was a hit-and-run fatality. A senior citizen unhappy in a care home. Weather highlights. People protesting a new condominium development. Alex would catch herself in the middle of a thoughtless trance, one hand squeezing the bandaged finger to the point of pain. She could be waiting for coffee to brew or a microwave to ding or for one of Sara's terrible programs to end. And Alex's mind would drift off a few feet out from where she stood. It wasn't meditative or serene. It was just mindless. And then Sara would ask for another program and Alex would take a deep breath and feel that ache in her left index finger as her other hand compressed it. "I said just one episode, Sara," Alex turned off the television. Alex loaded the washing machine, shut the door with an assertive thud, whisked open the tray for the soap and stared at the empty drawer, the white plastic glazed from water. She breathed in and out. Footsteps pattered from above. "Mommy," Sara asked and Alex turned, blinking, not sure how long she'd been standing still. It didn't feel like seconds or minutes; it didn't feel like anything. "Mommy," Sara repeated, urging her to come upstairs. Alex wanted to reach down and pick up her daughter, hold her tight, tell her how much she loved her right then. But Sara just wanted her mother to intervene in a sibling argument.

Alex took off her bandages, expecting them to have stuck to her skin like hardened glue, but instead the tube of spiraled Band Aids slid off with ease, revealing waxen skin stripped of pigment. Pressing back the tip of her finger, the serrated edges of the incision parted. It started to bleed. She should have gotten stitches. She secured another trio of bandages around with such force that the exposed fingertip swelled plum.

Alex's plans to see Tricia for a play date fell through mere minutes before she was ready to start the car. Caleb was already at soccer camp. Sara was already dressed. Tricia sent a text message that made it very clear that she hated cancelling but something had come up last minute. Although the details of this *something* were never explained, a colon and open-parenthesis were included to illustrate her disappointment.

Alex stood by the back door, watching the screen in the palm of her hand, doubting Tricia's sincerity, wanting to tell her not to bother with the sad faces. Now what?

The phone hummed and the screen lit up livid. Tricia added: *And crazy about Texas, huh?*

Alex turned on the television. At least one hundred people in the suburban town of Deer Park had killed themselves. The first reports were of individuals jumping from the roof of a three-story office building. What initially appeared to be a suicidal act became a most desperate attempt at self-preservation, as if people were choosing to plunge from the top of the building as opposed to remaining indoors for even another second. Witnesses assumed that there was a fire, that there was a terrorist on a rampage—that there was *something*—but when the first responders arrived, the building was vacant. Not a single person remained. Nothing burned. There were no signs of intruders. Chairs and tables were left upright. Doors were unlocked. Lights were on. The air was clean and uncontaminated. Inside the bland stucco building, nothing was out of the ordinary. Outside, a rectangular ring of corpses outlined the structure. As Alex sat on the sofa in front of the living room television, watching with piercing focus, none of the authorities had yet to give an explanation. There was no known video footage of the incident. One eye witness driving past described the victims as lemmings—they did not hesitate as they approached the edge of the roof, stepping into the abyss with limp arms. Alex turned from one cable news channel to another, hoping for some scoop, some footage, some insight.

But beyond the obvious fact that the entire populace of a suburban office building had leapt to their death, everything was conjecture. All other buildings in a two-mile radius were evacuated. When Sara demanded attention, Alex wasn't ready to leave the sofa. She started a movie on the downstairs television and told Sara she could watch the whole thing if she wanted. Alex then returned upstairs, one hand massaging her bandaged finger, watching shaky news coverage of *The Terror in Texas*, as it had now been christened. A man on the street told a reporter that he believed that this was some sort of terrorist attack perpetrated by the Chinese, that the incident from a few days back was a trial run. This was an act of war, people assumed. Perhaps using chemicals. Maybe even mind control. The hapless journalists could confirm nothing and so seemed content to let the ideas of the uninformed run wild.

When Hayden came home, Alex was listening to a speech from President Bush. His eyes winced with a deliberate, steely gaze. He called what happened in Texas an atrocity. Even though he could not yet confirm what had exactly happened, he assured the American people that the government and military were exploring all possible angles. He alluded back to the attacks on September Eleventh, reminding his citizens that Americans were resolute under pressure.

"You must have heard about Texas?" Alex asked without taking her eyes away from the screen.

"Of course. Do they have any idea what happened yet?"

Alex shook her head.

Hayden was about to walk into their bedroom when he recoiled, staring at Alex, not the television, "Jesus Christ, what are you doing?"

"I'm watching the news."

"No. Your finger."

Alex looked down. Her hands were covered in blood, smeared from her exposed left index finger, over the surrounding digits, down to the wrist and onto her other hand. The bandage lay on the rug by her feet, still cylindrical. When she turned her hands around to inspect them, she seemed to be waking up from a dream, her eyes reluctant to focus. She gasped. She didn't say a word.

Hayden asked, "Where is Sara? Caleb?"

Alex shook her head.

"Sara!" Hayden yelled. "Caleb!" He hurried out of the room and Alex could hear both of their voices. Sara was in her room. Caleb was downstairs. When Hayden returned to the living room, Sara was in his arms and he kissed her blonde tufts of hair in a way that seemed to imply that he wasn't going to give her back. He looked down at Alex, "Go wash your hands and put the bandages back on, for Christ's sake." Hayden then leaned over, grabbed the remote, and shut off the television.

"What happened to Mommy?"

"She just cut herself." Hayden kissed Sara again, his eyes focused on Alex. "Go. Go now."

They ordered pizza for dinner and ate around the dinner table. There was no conversation. Alex listened to the sticky smacking of Caleb's lips and Sara's insistent complaints about pepperoni being too spicy. Hayden then offered to take the kids to the park so that Alex could relax a little, take a bath, something, anything. The moment the front door closed, Alex turned on the television. There was now security camera footage from a neighboring building in Deer Park, showing what looked like shadowy bags of flour falling onto the pavement.

When the children were in bed, Hayden asked Alex to sit outside with him on the back deck. He started with: "Have you been drinking?"

"I haven't been drinking." Alex's tone and immediate reply made it clear that not only was she expecting this question, she was insulted by it. It didn't have to be the very first thing he asked.

"Well, you can't blame me for asking."

Alex wanted to tell Hayden that she figured that it was precisely within her rights to blame him for asking. Yes, her father drank too much. And so did her grandmother. There was a penchant for alcoholism in both sides of her family and that made his question all the more insulting. He had no fucking idea what it meant to have a parent with a "drinking problem." Even that phrase diminished the impact of the disease. People like Hayden couldn't understand what it was like to know from your earliest years that your own father, one of just two pillars which held up a child's entire universe, has an addiction. That he does things not because he wants to, but because he needs to, and that nothing you say or hope for will have any impact on his decisions. "Is that something that you're worried about? That I spend my days drinking alone?"

"I'm sorry—I didn't mean it like that."

"I don't drink on my own during the day. I'm not a desperate housewife."

"I said, I'm sorry." Hayden then shook his head. Alex knew that he was about to retract his apology. "Actually, no. I'm *not* sorry. I came home and you were on the couch with your hands covered in blood. You didn't even know what was going on. It was a fair question."

"So, was this why you wanted me to come out here? So that you can make me feel like shit?"

"I want to know what's going on."

"I told you already. Something happened."

Hayden grimaced. "What do you mean?"

"When I cut myself. I haven't felt right ever since."

"What are you talking about?"

"You never fucking listen, do you? Maybe if you weren't on your phone all the time you would have remembered."

"You cut your fucking finger. I think I understood."

"I didn't just cut my finger. Fuck, Hayden, I told you about this." Alex groaned and stood up. "I don't have the energy to fight tonight. I really don't."

"What happened when you cut your finger?"

"I was," Alex didn't want to repeat herself. Saying these things aloud made it sound more ridiculous. "Maybe you're right. Maybe I should go to the doctor. Maybe I'm losing my mind."

"I never said that."

"Ever since that moment I cut myself, I haven't felt," she put a hand up in the air as if to grab the appropriate term from some imaginary shelf, "*whole*. I feel like part of me is, I don't know, outside my grasp. I lose track of time. I squeeze my finger. I don't know." Alex knew that the first tear would swell up and over any second now. She hated the way she looked when she cried. Fragile and dependent. "I don't know what's going on, but I don't need you accusing me."

"Hey, hey," Hayden stood up and held her tight. Alex wanted to be held and yet hated the feeling that without Hayden she would fall apart. "I'm sorry. I was just scared when I came home."

26

"Trust me. I was scared, too."

It was now confirmed that one hundred and seventeen people died as a result of blunt force trauma in *The Terror in Texas*. Not a single person was unaccounted for—everyone went over the roof. There was no indication of any type of threat or persuasion. Nine people survived, workers who plunged onto the bodies of others and broke countless bones, punctured lungs, fractured skulls. The few that regained consciousness remembered nothing of the incident. There was no group claiming responsibility, there were no leads, there was not a single reasonable explanation for what had happened. Family members of the victims sobbed on camera, stating how their loved ones would never do something like this. Nothing made sense to them and they demanded answers. There was talk of all offices in the vicinity remaining shuttered for another day. Investigators in biohazard suits marched in behind the squadron of news cameras. Alex only turned off the television when she heard the squeaking floorboards warn of Hayden's imminent arrival. She slunk into bed just before he opened the door. Minutes later, Hayden's snores made it impossible for her to sleep and Alex thought of moving to the living room couch. There might have been an update on CNN. Then Sara awoke her at three in the morning. She'd had a nightmare about enormous, wild black ducks and yearned to come into bed with them, at which point Hayden groaned and said that he would sleep on the sofa. Sara rolled over and nudged Alex awake every half-hour. "What time is it?" she'd ask, as if she possessed a solid grasp on the conventions of the twelve-hour clock. "It's time to sleep," Alex replied each time. But then the sun was up. Hayden exited the house. She rolled over and looked towards the closed but radiant blinds and sighed, knowing that there was no more rest to be had. She said to Sara: "Go and play in the living room, I'll be there in a minute." Sara crawled out of bed and scurried across the hallway. All Alex desired was a few more minutes of rest. Sara then called out, demanding assistance with the television. "Yeah, yeah, I'm coming." Alex said and sat up, wishing that she could train her daughter to make coffee. If Sara knew to enter with a steaming cup in hand, then this this would greatly soften her demands.

"*Mommy!*"

Alex groaned, not looking forward to yet another day. She knew it was going to be a long one.

PART TWO

Alex didn't want to obsess. She wasn't going to leave the television on for more than a few minutes at a time. She had to make breakfast for the kids as well as pack a lunch for Caleb before dropping him off at soccer camp. She had to go grocery shopping with Sara before driving to Tricia's house for that rescheduled play-date. Should Tricia cancel it again, Alex would breathe a sigh of relief. This activity felt like a chore with everything else that she needed to do. She still had the children's laundry to wash, dry and organize. She had to return those stupid running shoes of Sara's that came apart within a week. And then she'd have to pick Caleb up before making dinner in anticipation of Hayden's return home. Every hour of the day was spoken for with tasks that required none of her passion and yet drained all of her spirit. She yelled downstairs, telling Caleb that he had to be ready in five minutes. Of course, he didn't reply and again she hollered, wanting to remind him just whose idea it was to enroll him in the camp. He pleaded for her to register him and now every morning felt like she was forcing him off to school. "You better have your shoes on in five minutes."

Alex hurried through stop signs, amber lights and slow left-hand turns towards the playing fields. Caleb asked to listen to Kanye but his request was turned down. He then asked for Justin Timberlake. Alex turned on the radio. Caleb repeated his demands and Alex reminded him that they would be there in a matter of minutes. It was only as they approached the park and its ambling parade of vehicles expelling jersey-clad children that Alex paid attention to what the DJ was saying. His voice was breathless, nervous. *"We are getting a lot of different reports here about incidents in different cities. Nothing has been confirmed, as far as I know, but I'm hearing about what seem to be terrorist attacks in Toronto, Seattle, New York, Los Angeles. These are just some of the North American cities that I'm hearing about, and online we're reading about other places all over the world. In Seattle, a panic has broken out downtown. There are reports of people fleeing from something but we don't have details as to about what—"*

"Bye, Mom." Caleb said, the slamming door a jarring gunshot. He ran along the sidewalk towards the other children. Alex's mouth hung open, wanting to say something to her son but not sure exactly what. He was already gone. He was talking to another boy. The announcer on the radio was describing something about a crowd of people jumping off bridges in New York. Hundreds. Maybe thousands. Sara started asking for music and Alex looked back towards the children. She could no longer see her son. A car honked from behind and Alex held up her hand in the rearview mirror, asking for forgiveness. She pulled up a few meters and then veered to the side. Sara repeated her demands and Alex wanted to tell her to shut up. Alex turned up the volume. The DJ was stammering. He admitted that he wasn't sure what there was to say. There seemed to be too much. Her heart raced. She looked down at her bandaged finger and remembered that feeling. This wasn't just in her head. They were at the precipice of something they couldn't see or appreciate. This was real.

"Mommy!" Sara demanded.

Alex snapped. "Shut the fuck up, Sara." Sara shut the fuck up. Alex shook her head, apologizing as Sara began to cry. She leaned back and grabbed one of Sara's hands. "I'm sorry. I'm sorry." Alex looked towards the children. Hundreds of them. Caleb was in there, somewhere. It was three minutes past nine in the morning, Pacific Daylight Time, of Tuesday, August 14th, 2007. The DJ wasn't saying a word. Alex squeezed Sara's hand. "Just wait here, babe. Wait here. Please. I'll be right back. I promise." Alex unclipped her seatbelt and stepped out from the vehicle. She could still hear Sara's cries in behind her. "Caleb!" she called out towards the mass of boys and girls, her tone one of a parent fearing abduction. Adults spun to face her as she repeated herself, looking over the bounding and jostling heads for her son's wavy, asymmetrical tufts of black hair. She loved that hair, that uncontrollable hair. She always resisted his demands to cut it too short. Attempts to tame if not raze the sumptuous chaos of his mane would make him like any other boy. Not her boy, not her son, not her Caleb. And there it was, that hair, a rising swell ready to whitecap.

"Caleb," She yelled and grabbed him by one shoulder. "We have to go."

"What?"

Alex pulled him away, gripping his outstretched left arm. "We have to go now."

"I just got here."

"We have to go." Parents watched them. Now she seemed to be the abductor. Adults whispered into each other's ears as they parted a clearing for Alex and Caleb. "Get in the car."

"I'm not going. "

"Get in the fucking car."

"What did I do?"

Alex looked up over Caleb and towards parents and children. She breathed so heavily that her chest heaved. If she really was losing her mind, then it was on display for hundreds of people. Someone walked towards her, a short man with a Bic-shaved head and a tentative, nervous smile. "Is everything alright?" he asked with one hand out, helping someone who'd fallen down.

"We're fine," Alex said.

"If there's anything I can do to help—"

"I said, we're fine. Get in the car, Caleb."

"I don't want to fucking go."

Alex slapped him, angry that he chose to swear in front of a stranger. She didn't want to look this man in the eyes. She knew what he was thinking. *What kind of family does this poor boy belong to?* She pulled open his door and pushed him in. "Now is not the time." Caleb conceded enough to be forced into the backseat. Sara was still crying, strapped in tight. Alex kept her head down while running around to the driver's side, shutting the door without looking another person in the eye. The radio was silent. She twisted up the volume but still heard nothing. She pulled out and drove into the serene residential neighborhood. Stately, century-old wooden homes with stained-glass windows, crisply painted trim and hedges cut with sharp corners stood proudly behind rows of arching, moss-draped trees. A man sprayed his glistening Audi sports car, which dripped frothy suds onto a driveway of patterned paving stones. White iPod headphones hung from each ear and he nodded to an unheard beat. Caleb was complaining the entire time, but Alex didn't reply. She pulled over and searched the radio for another station, something that was still broadcasting. From the crackling hiss emerged a woman describing a scene of bodies floating in a bay. The speaker was short of breath, as if running while speaking on the phone. *"There must be thousands,"* she said.

"MOM!" Caleb kicked the seat ahead of him to get her attention. Alex punched the volume knob to silence the radio. He asked, "What's going on?"

Alex didn't know what to say. Quite simply, she did not know what was going on. She just felt something. Felt something awful. And this was not a mood that could be ignored. This was the feeling a person has when learning of a loved one's death. Pure, inescapable, undeniable dread. But she didn't know why. Caleb asked again, now pleading as Sara's cries sank into sniffling whimpers. Alex was rubbing her finger. She pulled her hands apart and gripped them around the steering wheel. She then turned around to face her son. "Caleb, I'm sorry. But we have to go away from here. It's not safe."

"What happened?"

She struggled with what to say. "Remember 9-11?"

Caleb shook his head.

"But you've heard of it, right? Well, I think something like that is happening, right now. We have to go." Alex nodded. "We have to go." She was talking to herself. There was no time to remain still on a residential road. She pulled out and withdrew the cellphone from her pocket to call Hayden. "Fucking pick up," she muttered while disregarding stop signs.

He didn't answer and she tossed the phone onto the empty passenger's seat before flicking on the radio. A man described the situation in Seoul. It was just past two in the morning. Expressways were clogged with millions of people. There were reports of residents rising out of bed to attack one another, as if sleepwalking and deranged. People were tumbling off from towers all throughout the metropolis. When Caleb started listening, he stopped asking questions.

"Is this happening here?" he asked.

Alex pulled up to their house. Kids chased each other through the adjacent park, their parents sitting idle on a bench. "I don't know. Here," she passed her cell phone to Caleb. "Keep trying to call Dad. If you get a hold of him, come get me. Otherwise, stay in the car. I won't be gone for long."

"Where are you going?"

"Just inside to get a few things. But stay here." Sara called for her mother and Alex leaned over to squeeze her hand. "I won't be long. Caleb is going to stay here with you."

Alex ran inside her house and turned on the television while grabbing the landline to call her mother and Kevin. They didn't pick up. On the news, the caption read: *"Global Terrorist Attacks?"* The announcer narrated footage of an urban street in the evening, taken from a rooftop at least ten stories above the ground. Five-lane roads with flashing traffic signals and parked cars were littered with motionless bodies. Alex looked out the front window towards her SUV; Caleb and Sara were still inside. The phone in her hand rang. "Hello?"

"Well, good morning, Alex. We saw—" It was Barbara. She sounded tired but calm. Alex knew that they must have been in bed when she called.

"Mom, have you seen the news?"

"*No. We were sleeping still. What's wrong? What's happened?*"

"I don't really know, exactly. Something bad."

"*Alex, are you okay?*"

"I'm fine. Right now. I don't have time to talk. Turn on the news. I think we might come out to see you two."

"*What is going on?*"

"Just watch the news. Like I said, I don't have time. I'm glad you two are okay. I love you very much. Keep close to the phone. I will call again when we're on the highway."

"*You're coming out today?*"

"I think so."

"*Alex, are you okay?*"

"I said, I'm fine. But I have to go. I love you, Mom"

"*I love you, too.*"

"Okay." Alex hung up the phone. She walked to the front window and waved towards Caleb until he acknowledged her, his expression hidden behind the sun's glare. She dialed Hayden's number again. Looking outside, the day was perfect. The sky was a smooth, smoky blue. The wide leaves of the boulevard trees lazily rustled in the gentlest of breezes. Their hydrangeas in the front yard were blooming into great, dense balls of turquoise and teal. There were no sirens to be heard. There were no people fleeing along the sidewalk. There was no backlog of cars desperate to escape. It was an unspoiled Tuesday morning. The world before her appeared unchanged, unfazed by this news. Someone up the block was mowing the lawn. She was the one going crazy.

"Maybe I should stop?" Alex said to herself. "Maybe I should slow down? Maybe I should stop?" She felt each breath in and then out, guiding them, proving to herself that she was the one in control here. She looked through the window towards her two children, still in the car, still waiting. "Maybe you should think about this, Alex?" She put down the phone. She sat down on the sofa facing the television. The graphics at the bottom still read, *"Global Terrorist Attacks?"* This time she noticed the question mark. Not even CNN knew what to call this. There was footage of a street that looked familiar, perhaps in Greenwich Village. No one was talking. Nothing was being filmed. She closed her eyes, wanting to cry but refusing to let herself break down. "What am I doing? What am I doing?" She visualized those parents at the soccer camp, their pitiful expressions—a pity reserved exclusively for her two children. For her, they possessed nothing but contempt. Her lungs heaved, a single spasm, and she stared to cry. "Stop it." She wondered if she should bring Caleb and Sara inside. Apologize to them. Tell them that it's not their fault. Call back Barbara and Kevin. Admit to them that she's losing her mind. She closed her eyes and no longer fought back the tears.

Alex only heard a light, crackling static, the crinkling of paper in another room. She looked at the television and nothing had changed. The same graphics, that same street in New York City. The same question-mark. The same silence. No one was talking. No one was being interviewed. No one was visible from the supposedly live footage. She turned up the volume and there was nothing to hear aside from the static and a faint, droning whine. She thought the screen might have frozen but the headlines at the bottom changed. *Reports of thousands fleeing Houston.* She fumbled to change the channel. The network wasn't broadcasting. The screen was black. Out her window, a perfect Tuesday morning.

Alex ran towards her vehicle and opened the driver's door. "Have you gotten a hold of Dad?" she asked while taking back the phone. Caleb shook his head. Sara's cries had settled into quivering sniffles and Alex reached back to squeeze her hands. Caleb asked what was happening. "I don't know, exactly," she said. "But we have to get Dad. We have to go to the university." Even as Alex said these words, she questioned her own sincerity. Right then, they were just a couple of minutes from the highway. She could be one of the first out of the city. That was what matters, she knew. Timing. Every second counts. As she drove to the end of her narrow street, the decision was simple. Turn left, go to the highway and flee the city. Turn right, drive to the university and get Hayden. "Keep trying to call Dad. Don't stop."

The intersection was clear.

Alex turned right.

Now she could tell that something was happening. Cars sped past. People ignored red lights. Drivers gripped their wheels with tight fingers as if to keep them from getting away. And yet others glided past in convertibles, top down and singing. It was 9:21 in the morning according to the time on the dash. As the road descended beneath the highway, her eyes traced the paths of trucks that whisked past overhead.

Hayden worked fifteen minutes away at Simon Fraser University, a hulking post-modern jumble of exposed concrete buildings atop what people generously referred to as a mountain. Alex considered it a large hill. As she passed the weathered wooden sign welcoming people to campus, Hayden picked up his phone. *"Hey, Twelve-Missed-Calls. What's wrong?"*

"You don't know?"

"Alex, I just finished a class. What happened?"

Dozens of cars rushed down the hill. *You're going the wrong way!* said the expressions of passing drivers. "You haven't heard about anything? I see people fleeing the university right now."

"*Fleeing? What? Wait. Where are you?*"

"I'm coming to get you. Meet me by the bus loop. Be there as fast as you can. Just go."

"*Alex, what happened?*"

He needed to trust her, to stop asking questions, to get off the phone and haul his ass to the bus loop. He could be there in a minute if he just did what she requested.

Instead he asked more questions.

"*Alex, what the fuck are you doing?*"

"I don't know exactly."

There was no reply.

"Trust me—"

"*Alex, you're scaring me.*"

"Just fucking listen. Get out of there. Meet me by the bus loop. Traffic is going to get terrible anytime now."

"*Is Sara with you?*"

"Sara and Caleb are both with me."

"*You didn't send him to camp?*"

"I did, but." Alex pulled over at the bus loop. She didn't want to get into it. "Are you in your office?"

"*Yes, but—*"

She hung up. Students were hurrying past, phones to their ears. Alex turned around to face Alex and Caleb. "Listen," she began and they listened, watching her with absolute focus. But she didn't know what to do, let alone what to tell them. She thought of leaving them in the vehicle while running to get Hayden. But anything could happen. People were going to get desperate. An SUV with nothing but two young children would soon be too tempting to a person with nothing to lose.

"Mom?" Caleb asked.

"Come with me." Alex sprinted around the car and pulled Sara from her straps. "Caleb, keep up. No matter what happens, we can't become separated. I know you can keep up. Just don't lose us. Got it? Don't get distracted. Just stay with me and Sara."

Caleb nodded and Alex ran as fast as she could while carrying her daughter. All traces of the warm morning sunshine vanished as soon as they stepped inside. The brilliant natural light made way for an array of fluorescent tubes secured behind crusted translucent plastic covers. The hallway ahead appeared like a sketch composed in an art class to teach students the vanishing point of perspective—four lines towards an unseen convergence in the middle, rectangular concrete ribs framing the corridor at regular intervals. Every wall was composed of pebbled cement and splintered amber lumber. Every angle was orthogonal. The famed architect of this university was inspired by the permanence of ancient ruins and dazzled his admirers of the 1960's with monoliths of concrete, the stone of modernity. Now it felt like a tomb. Alex's phone started to ring but she ignored it, trudging up a winding stairwell with Sara gripping her shoulder. She passed a glass wall outlining a computer lab and every student within watched video streams from the monitors. Most were silent. Some were crying. Hayden's office was down the hall and Alex yelled his name before noticing that Caleb wasn't with her. She spun around and called for him, her voice now desperate.

"Mom," Caleb emerged from the top of the staircase.

Alex knelt down and expected him to hurry towards her. Instead, he sprinted past and into Hayden's arms.

"Hey, Cal." Hayden held up his son and squeezed him as if he hadn't seen the boy in months, his seething eyes locked upon

Alex's. "What are you guys doing here?" For the sake of his children, Hayden attempted to intone his words as if this was jovial, part of a surprise birthday party.

Caleb replied: "Mom said we have to go get you. It's like 9-11."

"Hayden," Alex put down Sara and stretched her tired right arm. "Have you seen what's going on now?"

"I've read a few things online, but—"

"Then we have to go. I saw that the traffic hasn't yet backed up on the highway. My car is down by the bus loop. Let's go."

Hayden was lost for words. Alex, Caleb, and Sara all looked up towards him. He expelled a single beleaguered laugh. "Caleb, can you wait out here for a minute with Sara while Mom and I talk in my office?"

"No." Alex was firm. "We don't have time for that. Just trust me. We have to go now."

"Alex, you are terrifying the kids, do you realize that?"

"This isn't in my fucking head, Hayden. We need to go now. Or if you don't want to go, I'll take them without you. You can stay, but we're leaving."

"Mom?" Caleb asked, although neither of his parents looked down.

Hayden's jaw clenched and his eyes glistened. Alex thought he might strike her and she welcomed the thought. *Fucking hit me, make it easy for me to leave.* He swallowed and cleared his throat. Alex picked up Sara. Facing his family again, Hayden exhaled and nodded. He licked his lips and started talking, "Alex—"

A chorus of people screamed from down the hall. Alex jogged towards the commotion, Sara in arm. Hayden called for her but she stopped by the computer lab. Few people sat, instead groups huddled around screens as the broadcast CCTV footage showed a mass of people, as dense and wide as fans streaming out from a stadium, charging across a multilane street devoid of cars, past a wide concrete walkway, and over a wrought-iron barrier into water. Bodies tumbled over the edge without hesitation, plunging down with relaxed limbs. No one pushed, no one shoved. No one looked back or around. No one tried to stop anyone else or struggled to veer out of line. Every single person hurried with great efficiency towards their demise.

"It's the Thames," Hayden said, placing a hand on Alex's shoulder. "That's right by St. Paul's."

Alex nodded. It didn't stop. She looked at the river. It was full of garbage, littered with thousands of black, motionless lumps. Students started to leave the lab, crying, their pace becoming frantic.

"What's going on, Alex?" Hayden asked.

"Mom?" Caleb was unable to see the computer monitors with all the people around. "What is it?"

"We should go." Alex said.

His hand squeezing Alex's shoulder, Hayden remained silent. She looked around, ready to repeat her demands, but now he nodded. The power went out and for a fraction of a second nothing could be seen, eliciting shrieks from the students crammed inside the computer lab. The emergency lights came on with a series of clicks.

"We should go," Alex repeated.

"But—"

Students ran past, jostling Caleb. A young man looked back, as if to apologize. His eyes locked onto Hayden's while staggering back, impatient to continue his escape. "Doctor Maclean," he said, mouth agape, ready to add something more but instead just nodded once and hurried onwards.

"Hayden?"

"Okay," he said, first as if surprised by his own reply before repeating himself, now with assurance. "Okay. I'll get my car."

"Let's not waste time. I'm parked just by the bus loop."

"Okay." He picked up Caleb and led the way towards the stairs. Alex took Sara and followed from behind. Once at the bottom, slivers of sunlight draped across the tiled floor. Now everyone hurried, phones out. *Hello? Hello? Are you there? Hello?* Pushing open a pair of exit doors, the mid-morning sun felt oppressive and searing compared to the catacombs of the university. Their tan SUV was just ahead, its lights on, engine running. "I'll drive," Hayden said after nearly throwing Caleb into one of the back seats.

"Fuck that," Alex said, passing Sara over. "Strap her in." This was not for debate. She was the one who awarded her family a head start. She was not about to pass over the reins.

Hayden didn't argue the point. He climbed into the passenger seat and Alex accelerated off before he'd closed his door. A fleet of busses remained parked, drivers standing in a group, shaking their heads, looking around and shrugging shoulders. Aimless passengers almost staggered, hands on their gasping mouths. Another car sped past, nearly careening into the fir and spruce trees that outlined the descending road as they left the campus.

"The network is down," Hayden said, holding up his phone. "No bars, nothing." He turned on the radio, searching for a station but finding only static on all frequencies, both A.M. and F.M. "What's going on?"

Alex shook her head. Such details seemed trivial at this point. All that mattered was that they had to get away. And no matter how fast Alex seemed to be driving, someone else was fleeing even faster.

So, she went faster.

"Careful, Alex." Hayden said, looking back towards the kids. Sara seemed exhausted, her eyes glazed and red but steady. She looked out the window to her right at the passing trees, sucking her thumb. Hayden reached back and patted Caleb's head, squeezed his hand. "You're doing good, Cal?" Through a break in the trees, he saw black smoke, several bands trailing up from the distance. "You see that?" He said to Alex, motioning with his chin and turning around to look.

"Where is that?"

"Maybe the airport?" A dense swath of trees blocked his view of the source, but the smoke wafted high into the clear sky before stratifying into horizontal layers, miles above the ground. "What was the last thing you heard, Alex?"

"You were there. Those people in London. I have no idea."

"Do you know if something happened here?"

"Not that I know. I heard a little about Seattle. I know that. And it's all over the place."

Traffic slowed at an approaching intersection. No matter how aggressively Alex wished to drive, she had to come to a stop. All directions had to contend with blank, powerless signals while a pair of collided cars remained crumpled and intertwined in the middle, their drivers standing close to their wrecks, talking with clasped hands atop their heads. Someone honked and one of these men held up a long, stiff middle finger to the mass of waiting vehicles. A motionless SkyTrain car loomed on the guideway that passed overhead, helpless passengers standing at the windows, gazing out.

"Mother—" Alex began, trying to peer around the cars for some opening that no one else had noticed. Every second counts, she knew. "Hold on." She veered around the vehicles ahead and charged into the intersection. Cars approached from both sides and Alex stomped on the gas. She just had to make it past the far crosswalk. She didn't look left or right. It didn't matter what she knew, only that she kept moving. If these other cars were going to hit, then it was already too late. Hayden gasped a curse and Alex kept her foot on the accelerator. The bold, white parallel lines of the crosswalk disappeared beneath the hood, under her wheels. The road ahead was open and clear.

"Jesus," Hayden yelled, looking back at both kids. "You're going to fucking kill us."

"Every second counts." This vacant road was a gift that could not be wasted. The exit for the highway was ahead. The overpass reached over all eight lanes and the traffic below still moved. She merged in and kept up with the flow. Hayden looked out towards the sky, the embankment on either side blocking his view of the rest of the city, and then glanced back to the kids. Sara still sucked her thumb. Caleb stared straight ahead, his skin flushed.

Hayden then fiddled with the radio again, his breaths still heavy. "How can I not pick up anything?" he said, resistant to the silence. "There must be something, somewhere."

Alex didn't reply. A sign advising her of their usual exit hurtled past. She would not turn her neck but watched Hayden in the blurry edge of her vision. His eyes remained aimed at the dash, his head cocked so that one ear was close to a speaker.

"There's always something."

The right lane split apart but Alex remained steadfast, the steering wheel unmoving in between her fingers. The interior of their SUV flickered dark as they passed through the shadow of an overpass. Hayden still twisted the tuner on the radio. She waited for him to comment. To notice.

"Wait?" Hayden sat up and looked back. "Where are we going? We just missed our exit."

"We're going to my mother's."

He stalled, processing Alex's statement as if conducting a slow translation. He must not have heard her correctly.

"We're going where?"

"Barbara and Kevin's."

"That's a nine-hour drive."

"It'll be safe there."

"I thought we were going home?"

"We have to get out of the city."

"We never discussed any of this."

"Because there's no time to discuss. Every second counts."

"But we don't even know what's happening. Don't you think it might be safest at home, where we have our things?"

Alex shook her head. This was nonnegotiable. "Whatever is happening, the farther we are from cities, the better."

"Alex, fucking listen to yourself."

"We can't go home. Look, look. All around us, the traffic is still moving. Soon it won't. We have to go while we can."

"Alex, you need to listen to me. We have to make these decisions together."

"Not about this. I know."

"No, you don't. You told me you don't know what's happening."

"I don't know what's happening but I know we have to leave. I know that."

"How do you know?"

"Because," Alex rubbed the bandage of her left index finger with the adjacent thumb. "Why can't you just fucking trust me?"

Hayden didn't respond.

"Just fucking trust me." The tangerine metal latticework of the Port Mann Bridge approached and the highway ascended the sprawling, meandering Fraser River. She switched to the rightmost lane in order to get a clear view over the edge. The murky water was a smoky moss, especially calm, a gentle lake hundreds of meters below. Strands of idle log boons remained still, moored to anchors. Two dozen rows of railroad tracks framed the far shore where shunting locomotives expelled churning diesel fumes and idle lines of boxcars resembled necklaces drawn taut and arranged in parallel rows. There was nothing unusual. No bodies. No panic. She looked out downstream, towards the city that bunched up against the north bank, the distant bridges hazy and lacking color or texture. There seemed to be no sign of anything unusual. Not even those trailing pillars of smoke could be seen. Just a quiet morning on a Tuesday in August. A beautifully calm and quiet summer morning.

Hayden looked back towards the city before it disappeared from view upon reaching the southern embankment, stands of evergreen trees rising up from either side of the highway. He asked, "Are you sure about this, Alex? How do you know we aren't overreacting?"

"I'm not sure of anything."

"Maybe we should turn around?"

"If I'm wrong, then I'm wrong. Then we drove out of town just because."

He looked at his phone and resumed scanning the radio frequencies. "What's been going on?"

"That day I cut myself, I felt something. I told you, I felt something, a presence. Like I was on the edge of being enveloped. Like someone else was watching me, or controlling me. I haven't felt the same since. I haven't felt right since. And at times, that feeling comes back. Sometimes just a little. Sometimes it's overwhelming. And I've been feeling it all morning. I just feel it."

"Even now?"

"Yes. I think. I don't know." Alex shrugged. "It's not tangible. I don't even know. It's not obvious until it's over." She looked towards him. "Do you have any idea what I'm talking about?"

An announcer, garbled and distorted, emerged from the radio's static before vanishing. "Did you hear that?" Hayden twisted back, notch by notch, trying to find the A.M. station. The voice returned, that of a woman, her voice anxious and yet monotone, a grade-school student reading before a disinterested class. *"I want you to understand that whatever I did, whatever apologies I have to make, I make them now. I want you to understand that I love you and that I always will love you, even if you are gone, even when I am gone. I want you to know that I am sorry that I couldn't be there with..."* The woman's voice descended beneath a wave of white noise but resurfaced seconds later. *"I am lonely and frightened right now, but I will keep talking. I will keep talking because maybe you can hear me. Maybe you are listening and hearing ... some moment of clarity, of calm in this otherwise terrifying..."* Hayden waited, adjusting the frequency ever so gently, one, two, three silent clicks to the left, then to the right. The woman didn't return, buried beneath the static.

"What was that?" Alex asked.

"I have no idea. I've lost the signal." Hayden resumed searching the bandwidth, step by step, now sure that he could find something else.

Alex cursed. "Traffic is getting worse." The highway ahead became a string of blushing taillights. Within seconds they would come to a standstill. The next exit was still a few hundred meters ahead. "We have to get off of this road. We're going to be trapped."

"If the highway is packed then all the other roads will be worse."

"Maybe we can go through the States?"

"I don't think going through the border is going to save us any time," Hayden said before grabbing hold of another radio signal. It was music. Gentle and melodic jazz: piano, drums, double bass, trumpet. Hayden looked up to Alex, expecting this to be a mistake, a brief interlude, a theme song. Turning up the volume, one could hear the clicks and crackle of a vinyl record. The bass and horns backed off, revealing the sparkling twinkle of soft, braided cymbal hits. "Why is a station still playing music?"

Alex wasn't listening. She'd come to a halt. The cars behind her came to a halt. The only open space was the highway's shoulder to her right. She nudged the SUV over and then pummeled her steering wheel with the heel of one palm. "Fuck," Alex muttered, feeling that what little control of the situation she had was now gone. "I should get into the shoulder. Drive to the exit and down to the border. It's just a few minutes from here."

"Just wait." Without saying another word, Hayden opened

his door, stepped out and walked towards the next vehicle. Sara asked where he was going and Alex shook her head. Hayden motioned to the driver of the car ahead, holding up a fleeting wave with one hand before asking unheard questions. Other people started leaving their vehicles, looking up the highway, tapping on windows. The once crisp morning sun was building into a steady, sharp and unflinching heat. Hayden returned with a glistening forehead, the hairs above his ears a sodden pewter. He left the door open as if ready to flee with a moment's notice.

"What were you asking them?"

"Just what they know." Hayden said, shaking his head. "But they don't know anything. Nothing more than us. They saw that footage from London. And about something in Mexico. They're a family. Got two kids, probably four and five. They didn't seem to want to talk about it in front of them but I don't think they know anything. They were planning on going camping anyhow. They just left a few hours earlier than intended."

"That's a good idea," Alex said.

"What? Camping?"

"Talking to people." Alex opened her door, stepped out and lifted herself up on the tips of each shoe. As far as she could see, cars were stalled. A pickup truck grumbled past them along the shoulder towards the exit, inches from the side of their SUV, two of its wheels in the ditch and causing the entire vehicle to slouch on a sharp angle. Engines idled as people remained unwilling to accept the extent of the congestion, exhaust pipes rattling, dripping. The few cars that travelled westbound blurred past with haste, secure behind a taut wire barrier that precluded anyone from escaping this gridlock. As Alex walked between vehicles, never once did she hear music.

Everyone sat in silence, watching.

"Excuse me," a man asked from behind. He was young, surely still in his twenties, and the first thing she noticed was his hair—styled into a deliberate peak, a tuft of thick frosting on a cake. It seemed incongruous with the scenario around her. "Where are you coming from?"

Alex pointed behind her. "We came from New West— SFU, actually. Why's that?"

"I wasn't sure if you saw anything, if you came from Vancouver."

"Did something happen there?"

"Don't know. I was talking to a friend downtown on my phone when the network cut out. He said that people were panicking but I don't know if that's just because of what they saw on the news." He looked out over the hoods of the countless vehicles. "Some other people I just talked to said that a few planes crashed at the airport."

"We saw smoke from around there."

"Feels weird, though. Right? No one I asked knows what's going on. So, why are we all driving away? If there was a terrorist attack here, how do we know that going east is best?" He looked towards the vacant westbound lanes. "Shit, I mean, those lanes are empty. Totally empty. They're never empty."

The man had a point. The opposing lanes were now completely devoid of any traffic. This was the most vital connection in and out of the metropolitan area. Even in the dead of night, it should never be this quiet. She wanted to say more to this man, but couldn't think of the words. She walked between idle cars towards the median, gripping one hand around the woven metal wire, and stared down the unfilled lanes. The only movement was that of distant people whose marching figures quivered against the warm pavement. She thought of walking towards them. But it didn't make sense. There should be headlights. None of this made sense and she felt that she should be terrified and yet she only observed. The well-groomed man was standing adjacent to another car, his knuckles rapping against the glass, first a pair of rapid taps, then slow, slugging thuds. Nothing happened. The window didn't roll down. He remained hunched, looking in. His hand lingered in midair. Alex wondered why the man didn't move on. He stood still, not saying a word, and then straightened his back, looked up the highway. Alex continued to stare at that window that he'd knocked on. Through glare she could make out an ear and tufting, dark hair above. The ear and hair didn't move, staring forward, hands on the steering wheel, fingers motionless. She stared down to her shoes. There were feet beside her. Bare feet in leather sandals. Following up a pair of hairy calves revealed an athletic man in a shorts and T-shirt standing adjacent. He gazed forward, his eyes glassy and unfocussed. She wanted to ask him what he was doing, what he was looking at. But she didn't. She was sure she could, but she didn't. He brushed past her and walked down the crowded highway. She figured she should follow him. And that's when she realized that she'd been here before.

She remembered the patter of blood off the lip of the kitchen counter. She clenched her left hand and looked around. At least a dozen people stood outside their cars, staring as if stuck in time and then traipsing forward. She'd catch herself caught on details—a dried white bird dropping on a windshield that resembled the continent of Africa, the swirling exhaust from a tailpipe that wafted into the air like steam from a kettle—before reminding herself that she'd been here before.

She knew this feeling. She looked through the windshield of her SUV and Hayden watched the scene ahead, daydreaming. Sara and Caleb remained hidden beneath the sun's reflection. She turned back around again to face the highway. Up ahead, she could see a crowd. People were outside of their cars, hundreds of them. They weren't fleeing; it was quite the opposite. They seemed to be running into one another, filling in all the empty spaces, climbing up and over other vehicles. She wanted to keep watching, she wanted to run towards them and find out what was happening. After all, everyone else seemed to be getting a head-start. Alex just watched, not making a sound, slowly inching closer. She remembered looking at the sides of her left index finger, pulled apart wide like the unfurling of a tight zipper. She tried to tell herself to focus and her lips parted but she didn't make a sound. She clenched her hands and said aloud: "Focus, focus, focus." She tried yelling but it came out as a trembled croak: "Focus." She returned to her SUV, knowing that she was still in control but not for how long. She was repeating this word when she sat back behind the steering wheel. Hayden didn't ask what was going on or why she was talking to herself.

"We have to get out of here," Alex said, slowly, reading lines phonetically, words from another language. Hayden didn't respond. "Hayden, listen to me." With each word, she felt more in control. She knew the script. She knew the language. "Hayden," she wanted to yell but couldn't. She tried to slap him across the cheek. "Hayden, we have to go." He nodded. She shifted out of neutral and turned towards the shoulder. Depressing the gas sent their SUV lurching into the bumper of the car ahead, the force shoving everyone into their seatbelts.

"What?" Hayden asked, his eyes slow to look towards Alex.

"What are you doing?"

"We have to go. We have to go." She tried forcing her way through, pressing harder onto the accelerator and turning, nudging the other vehicle forwards hardly a foot. Heads turned but no one stepped out. Alex backed up and tried again, clearing the obstruction but nearly driving into the ditch before veering left, wheels sliding over the long stalks of sunflower grass that rose from the edge of the asphalt. She depressed her foot and sped ahead, her left side-view mirror clipping another car and breaking free. She gripped the steering wheel as tightly as she could and yet it seemed to slip away from her. Metal squealed like fingers down a chalkboard as she slid alongside another pair of cars.

"What are you doing?" Hayden repeated, his words calm. She wanted to let go. She wanted to allow her vehicle to take them off into the embankment. But the shoulder widened into a lane of its own. She had room now to swerve without hitting other objects but had to contend with a looping, winding off ramp. She gazed out towards the eastbound highway and a crowd was jostling, combative, and discolored. It didn't make sense. Everything was red. Red bodies, red hoods, red windshields, red streaks along the sides of tall, motionless semi-trailers. Her left headlight shattered against a concrete barrier and Alex brought her eyes back to the road ahead of her. Sparks abated as she twisted the wheel right, moving off the ramp and onto a straight, two lane agricultural road. In the other direction, cars lined up to merge onto the highway but she was the only person heading south. People walked along, outside of their vehicles, towards the melee. Hayden was saying something again, he was repeating himself again, but Alex kept watching the road, going faster. She could feel the grip of the steering wheel. She could feel her breaths in and out. She'd stood up too quickly but now her senses were returning. She could hear the whining, trembling engine. She shot through an intersection so quickly that she nearly clipped another car. She looked at the dash and she was going 160 km/hr. She stared at the arrow of the speedometer, not yet sure what it meant, not yet. It was that same struggle to recall the right word. 170 km/h. It was on the tip of her tongue.

"ALEX!" Hayden yelled. A car was turning into her lane. They were in free fall. Then Alex knew. She needed to take her foot off the gas. She needed to brake, but with a gentle tap. She pummeled her horn, fearful of losing control. She wanted to close her eyes as they careened past. The face of the other driver flashed past her like a single flickering frame in a movie. Two eyes and a dull face spliced into footage of a blurred road. She made it through. She was slowing down. She was regaining control. But she didn't want to stop.

"What," Hayden asked, his eyes wide but lost. "What is going on?"

Alex was going to say, *I don't know.* Instead she said nothing. She passed a sign informing drivers that the Aldergrove border crossing was one kilometer ahead.

"Alex, what happened?"

There was no traffic in either direction.

"Alex, why don't we stop for a moment?"

"No," she felt certain about this. They needed to keep moving. She remembered that image from the highway as they ascended the off-ramp. What must have been thousands of people, milling like livestock but covered in blood. It didn't make sense, but that was what she remembered.

"Alex—"

"Did you see that on the highway? All the people? All the—"

"What," Hayden began, ready to express his bewilderment. But he paused. There were signs urging motorists to slow down and to have their passports ready for inspection. Alex drove over a speed bump and the car rattled violently, the asphalt scraping the undercarriage. She apologized but didn't slow down. A sign encouraged people to turn right into the duty-free shop to purchase premium spirits and chocolates. The border control booths were empty. The barriers up. Alex drove through, only slowing to avoid ruining the car's shocks as they jostled over more speed bumps. Welcome to the United States of America. They drove down a rural road, leafy agricultural fields on either side. Mount Baker towered over the green foothills to the east, its imposing, flat-topped peak lathered in crisp, white snow. There were no signs of the city, the suburbs, the gridlock just behind them. This was pastoral and secluded. The 49th parallel was a portal through which they'd passed into a different world.

"Alex," Hayden's words were tender. "Please stop."

There were no other vehicles, no other people. They passed a derelict and weathered wooden barn, the boards sagging and silver. Parallel power lines drooped from lanky wooden crosses that traced one side of the country road. Although she didn't feel safe, Alex felt that she could pause for a moment, for a minute. She pulled over onto the narrow shoulder and let go of the steering wheel, her fingers unfurling, the joints sore. Hayden grabbed onto her hands. Twin headlights approached. A pickup truck roared past, nearly in the middle of the road and close enough to shudder their SUV. It seemed to wake her up. She looked into Hayden's eyes and asked with a heaving, throaty whisper: "You saw that, didn't you? As we came off the highway?"

Hayden exhaled, almost a sigh, lost for words.

"Daddy," Caleb asked, sounding short of breath. "Where are we?"

Alex turned around, so grateful to see both of her children in the backseat. It was as if she had forgotten about them—not just that they were with her, but that they existed. She wanted to pull Sara out from her spot and take her into her arms. The girl muttered a weak, "Mommy," and Alex's lungs quivered. She was so grateful to see her right there.

"Why are you crying, Mom?" Caleb asked.

"I'm just happy."

"You don't look happy."

Alex laughed and sniffled. "You're probably right." She glanced back to Hayden. He was still holding her right hand. Each seemed to wait for the other. His usually cocky grin was fragile. The more he thought to himself, the more he seemed to grow terrified. He swallowed and squeezed tightly before letting go.

"We probably shouldn't wait here too long."

Alex nodded. Flickering headlights drew her eyes to the rearview mirror. There was no sideview mirror. A vehicle approached, swinging into the opposing lane to pass. Alex looked to Hayden. She lowered the window and looked back, waving her hand out as a navy-blue pickup with Washington State plates blurred past. An elderly man and a woman were looking at her. That's all she could tell. The truck continued down the road, turning back into the appropriate lane. Its brake lights then illuminated and the rear tires wavered on the pavement before coming to a stop.

"Okay, then." Alex shifted into drive and caught up, lowering Hayden's window to line up with the driver of the pickup, a man who appeared to be in his sixties with a horseshoe of white hair that made his forehead appear unnaturally long, his pupils sheltered beneath heavy, drooping eyelids. The passenger, a woman with short, wavy strawberry blonde hair and ashen roots had been crying, still rubbing her eyes with the undersides of each wrist.

"Hey," Hayden said, leaning out the window, looking up and down the road. "Are you guys okay?"

The man kept both hands on the steering wheel. "I think so," he said, staring into the rear of Alex and Hayden's car, noticing the children. Their presence seemed to soothe him. "Do you know what's going on?"

Hayden shook his head before saying a word. "No. We were hoping that you could tell us something."

"We were just," the man's eyes darted towards Caleb and Sara. "I don't want to talk about it right now."

"Where are you heading to?"

The man looked to his wife. He turned back to Hayden. "We have place up near Mount Baker. Where are you all heading?"

Hayden shook his head. "We don't really know."

"Well, if you want, you're welcome to come with us for the night. We don't have much. It's nothing fancy, but there's space for a few other people."

Hayden looked to Alex. To him, it seemed obvious.

Alex nodded. "We might take you up on that."

"Well then, follow us. But we should go." He raised the window and inched forwards. Alex took a deep breath. She was going to let someone else take the lead for the first time that day. The pickup accelerated. Alex wasn't moving. She was going to, she knew that much, but first she needed just one more moment, one more second where she was the one in control. Before Hayden might make a comment, she hit the gas.

PART
THREE

Brent and Gillian's home was a half-hour drive away, built upon a clearing up a weaving road that cut a crevasse through the canopy of alpine trees. As she followed, Alex saw only one other vehicle on the highway, a hatchback with a single occupant traveling west. The driver made eye-contact with Alex but passed by too quickly for her to discern anything else. She parked their SUV on a patch of mossy gravel beside an empty boat trailer. Forested mountains obscured every horizon and Alex couldn't tell which direction she was facing when she stepped out, surprised by her staggering legs, the muscles of each exhausted as if she'd ascended this mountain on foot. Hayden and the children climbed out, directed by Brent and Gillian to follow them inside, and Alex was reluctant to walk away from her vehicle. What at first appeared to be a humble A-frame cabin opened up with the downward slope of the clearing into an expansive two-story house that overlooked an evergreen valley. The living room was rustic and yet felt vast and airy; a wall of trapezoid windows extended up from the hardwood floor into sharp peaks that traced the exposed ceiling.

A black leather recliner with cracked white indentations in each of the wide armrests was positioned in the middle, facing the balcony. Brent called it the Captain's Chair. Presumably, he was The Captain. The two bedrooms on the lower level were reserved for guests, both with pairs of twin beds pushed to opposite sides and ornate wooden nightstands in between, each detailed with brass fixtures. A third room housed only piano and a futon draped with knitted quilts. Caleb traced dark rose lines in the dust upon the varnished wood and Hayden's fingers glided along the smooth ceiling. "Here," Gillian said, motioning to pressed and hung children's clothes that occupied a quarter of a closet. "I thought your boy might want something more comfortable to change into." Caleb was still in his soccer jersey. Alex thanked her and minutes later Caleb was dressed in a Seattle Seahawks T-shirt with baggy overcast gray sweatpants that were translucent in the knees.

The power was out and their landline didn't work. Brent wanted to sit down and offered Hayden a glass of scotch. He appeared calm as he poured those first drinks, his hands steady, breaths deliberate. He descended into his recliner and looked out the windows. He didn't say a word. Within a minute, he'd finished his drink and stood up to pour himself another. Alex opened the French doors that led to the wooden balcony and took the kids outside. She kept Sara in her arms while Caleb wrapped his hands around the wooden spindles and stared out towards the calm, coniferous forest. It was all so tranquil, so beautiful, and somehow it didn't feel appropriate; this was a trick.

"Where are we?" Caleb asked and Alex wished that she could give him an answer. After hesitating, she admitted that she didn't know. Caleb asked who these people were and after a truncated laugh, Alex repeated herself. "I don't know." It was when Caleb asked what was happening that Alex remembered those people on the highway, what must have been a thousand strangers tearing into one another, a frenzied orgy of violence and yet somehow calm, orderly, dutiful. Alex held back tears as she returned inside and asked Gillian if there were any toys around that the kids could play with. Gillian apologized as if being an inconsiderate host and took the children downstairs to a storage room with boxes full of Lego and wooden train tracks.

"Do you mind if they bring the toys upstairs?" Alex asked, "I don't want them to be out of my sight." She then looked towards Brent. "And if you don't mind, I think I might really enjoy a drink, as well."

The adults sat in the living room, eyes ambling between the children and the idyllic scene out through the windows, where golden moss hung from the branches of evergreen trees like tinsel. The only voices were that of Caleb and Sara, each uncharacteristically complacent with each other's company, their quarrels and quips never lasting more than a couple of seconds. Alex joked that she hadn't ever seen them play this well together. Everyone else chuckled but offered nothing in return. Brent asked Hayden to come outside with him to the deck, implying that he didn't want the children to hear what they were going to talk about. While he was at it, Brent topped up both of their drinks and they stood out of earshot, their glasses resting on the railing. Alex didn't care for the insinuation that the women would be best to stay indoors. She said to Gillian, "Do you mind if I go outside?"

It was only as Alex stood, awaiting a response, that Gillian realized she had been asked a question. Her right hand gripped a glass filled an inch high with tap water, her thumb caressing it back and forth. She shook her head, grimaced as if having been rude. "Oh, yes. Of course. I'll stay here. I just want to sit."

Brent watched Alex as she stepped out, nodding as if to accept her admission. "It's beautiful here," Alex said, motioning out towards the forest. "It feels like we're thousands of miles from anywhere. Thank you."

Although seemingly ready to reply, Brent instead nodded and looked out towards the panorama without his eyes focusing on any detail, as if the view had long become so familiar that it was mundane, indistinct chatter in behind a conversation. He sipped from his drink and it clattered when put back down onto the railing. He then said to the treetops, not to any person in particular: "What the hell is happening?" Neither Alex nor Hayden could answer. Brent cleared his throat. "We were driving back from Seattle. That's where Garrett, our son, lives. We usually listen to the radio—we always listen to the radio—but we didn't. Gillian and I had a bit of an argument. Doesn't even matter what it was about now, does it? We weren't talking and we didn't turn on the radio and I just drove back home. But I took the wrong damn road without even realizing it. Usually take the 542 but we took the 539. We were going the wrong way and I knew it, but I kept driving. Remember thinking, 'We should get off,' and yet I didn't do anything about it. I don't know why I didn't swerve right off the road. I wasn't focused. I just kept driving." Brent looked inside, towards Gillian. She remained motionless on the sofa. "Then she screamed. Gillian. I heard her scream. It woke me up. She was looking behind her and in the rearview I saw all the cars trailing us—maybe five, maybe ten—veer off the road at the same time, right at full speed. They went into the ditches. Into the damn trees. One went into someone's home. One crashed into an electrical pole. Enough force to knock the whole damn thing down. I remember a jeep flipped, tumbled over and over like a toy. No way anyone survived that. Must have been going seventy, eighty. And I could feel it in me—that need to turn off to the side. It was like," he put his hands up in the air, gripping the imaginary wheel, "It like gravity was pulling me one way. It felt natural. But it was Gill's screams that kept me going straight. That kept me awake. I hit the gas, went as fast as we could. We turned on the radio and only found a couple of stations working. Said something about a terrorist attack. I don't know. We kept losing the signal. We tried to call Garrett, my son, but our phone wasn't working. We saw no one else on the roads. Nothing. And then we realized that we'd gone too far. Were almost in Canada. I turned us around and that's when we saw you all parked on the side of the road." Brent looked at Alex, his eyes bloodshot and glazed. "Seeing someone else, it gave us hope. Couldn't get a hold of anyone and then we saw you. You guys saved us."

They spent the afternoon sharing what they knew and then repeating those same recollections, searching for missed details or clues that they'd passed over before. Phones were left on a tabletop, powered on and facing up, and Alex checked for reception every few minutes. The entire house was calm and tired, minutes passing by without any words exchanged. Alex would catch herself staring out the window, her thoughts empty. Caleb asked to play the piano and his fumbled chords hummed through the floor. When the evening sun cut amber lines along the hardwood floor, Brent passed out in his Captain's Chair, chin buried into his sternum. Sara fell asleep on a loveseat and

Gillian watched her with an almost tearful smile. She then lit candles around the cabin and Hayden found Caleb on the futon, eyes closed, his legs folded up to his chest and a pink quilt covering only his shins and feet. Hayden carried him to the adjacent bedroom, laying him down on a bed across from Sara. Gillian went to her room soon after, her voice ragged and exhausted as she attempted to move Brent from his spot. After a couple of tepid tugs, she gave up and left him there, assuring Alex and Hayden that they could continue talking, that her husband could sleep through anything. He was just stressed and had a few too many drinks. Alex and Hayden sat out on the deck, the canopy of pointed treetops lit as if by a pale fluorescent bulb. The stars were so crisp and vivid that the expanse of the Milky Way became lush. It reminded Alex of her mother's place on Kootenay Lake. Then she'd think of her thirty-second phone call that very morning. Barbara had just woken up. She had no idea. Alex promised that she was going to call again once on the highway. She looked at Hayden's iPhone in her hand. The battery was getting low. No reception. She thought of her mother trying to call back, so confused, so scared. She should have spoken longer. Every second counts— yes—but what if those were her last seconds? Alex started tearing up and she knew she had to stop. If she let herself cry now it could go on forever, because surely there was so much more to feel sorrowful about than just one seventy-year-old woman?

"I'm going to go to the car to check the radio. See if I can pick up anything." Hayden said before offering for Alex to come with him. She declined, not wanting to be left alone on the deck but equally not wishing to return to that vehicle. She followed him through the candlelit living room—Brent was snoring in slurping bursts—and went down to see Caleb and Sara. The candles had gone out and Alex had to hold out her hands against the walls, fingers slithering against the paint. Her shin nudged the corner of one bed and she ran a hand down the mattress towards her daughter's knee. Crawling up beside her, Alex slid her thighs snug within the crook of Sara's legs. The girl rustled and reached out. Alex shushed as if Sara was still an infant, her lips in the girl's tangle of hair, kissing the back of her head between each breath, her hand gripping Sara's delicate fingers, and told her that it was okay, they were fine, she was not going anywhere, she could go back to sleep. Alex was tired and couldn't imagine going anywhere else. She would sleep on this twin bed in a contortion throughout the night, her nose buried in Sara's ringlets of hair, seeing nothing but her senses tickled, sheltered.

The world lit up with the washed-out strobe of a camera's flash. Alex opened her eyes and the room was pitch black. Sara didn't notice. No one else seemed to be in the room. Alex didn't want to wake up the children and lowered her head, closing her eyes slowly. Another flash blared through the lids of her eyes and she sat up. Sara rolled over and Alex looked around, unable to see anything. "Hayden?" she whispered. She heard no reply, no footsteps, nothing at all. She wouldn't lie down this time. And then she saw it with her eyes open, a searing white flash through the stout window between the two beds. She stood up and parted the horizontal blinds with two fingers, looking out over a sloping gravel path and towards the moonlit trunks of trees. It seemed obvious that it must have been lightning, except that there wasn't a cloud in the sky, not a rustle of a breeze. She gazed up, the blinds clattering against the window. She could see stars. Then the sky flashed white, a throbbing, silent blast over the treetops. If this was lightning then there should have been thunder. She stepped back from the window and when the room lit up again she could make out the still image of Caleb on his side, his face into his pillow, eyes closed. She heard footsteps. Through the closed door, Hayden called for her with an urgent whisper and she left the room, her hands guiding her along the walls between bursts of light. He stood atop a flight of stairs at the end of the hallway, waving her over. Cool air trickled down from the entranceway in behind him and the next flash rendered him a flinching silhouette as she climbed the steps.

"What is that?" Alex asked

"I don't know. Follow me." He rushed through his words, leading Alex out onto the dewy grass in front of the house. Their SUV was idling, the inside appearing candlelit in the surrounding darkness. Hayden craned his neck upwards towards the rash of stars in the sky, pointing. Right on cue, it lit up, a pulse of light that exposed all the details of the surrounding forests for no longer than the blink of an eye. Alex listened for something but all she heard was the idling engine of the vehicle and the ambling sway of the surrounding trees.

Hayden said, short of breath, "It's consistent. About every twenty seconds." He carried on counting under his breath. When he reached nineteen, the sky lit up once again.

"What the fuck could that be?"

Hayden shook his head, still counting.

"Do you hear a thing?"

Hayden pointed right as the sky lit up. "Nothing."

Alex pointed over the ridge of trees. The light seemed to radiate from a specific direction. "Which way is that?"

"I'm not sure."

"What could be making so much light but not make a sound? We should hear something, right?"

Hayden shrugged.

"You didn't get a radio signal anywhere?"

"No. I searched for a few minutes before this started."

"You should turn it off. Save the gas."

Hayden nodded and twisted off the ignition. He swung the door shut, startling Alex. The sky flashed and Hayden put his hands on her shoulders. She wanted his hands there, she wanted to feel his grip, his warmth, and she stepped back towards him. He held her tight and his chin rested on one shoulder. She flinched when the next flash came, right on schedule. Hayden counted under his breath. She looked at him and his eyes were glazed, presumably filled with wonder. "How are you so calm?"

"I'm terrified."

Alex grabbed his arms by the elbows and pulled them. She wanted to hear that. She wanted to know that he was frightened. And yet she wanted him to keep holding her. He couldn't keep her safe—she knew that much—but he could keep her warm, keep her close. "What is going on?"

"I think we might have to stop asking that question."

"I feel like we're stuck in a dream."

"I've thought that many times."

"I just want to wake up."

Hayden kissed her just below her right ear.

Alex repeated, feeling her lips quiver. "I want to wake up, back home, with Sara, with Caleb."

"I know."

"Why can't I wake up?"

Hayden kissed her again and gently shushed. She found it

both consoling and yet infuriating. She wiped her eyes and looked towards the open door of the house.

"Let's go to the deck," she said, forcing herself out from Hayden's grasp but keeping hold of his hand, pulling him with her. "Maybe we can see something else from up there." As they climbed the stairs to the living room, another flash revealed Brent's unmoved body on his armchair, black crescent shadows framing the bags beneath each eye. He was a corpse that reminded Alex of her father. The painless ease with which he could ingest such strong liquor. That panting, muted exhale of relief after a hoarding gulp. No matter how much he drank, he never seemed drunk. Just drinking. Alex recognized the expression on Gillian's face as Brent refilled his glass. Her eyes trailed his hands, her lips tight, ready to say something but never—ever—muttering a word. Alex stood within reach when the next flash exposed his parted lips, the mass of skin bulging out from beneath his chin. The drooping, haggard face of someone insulated from reality. Not dreaming, not thinking, not doing anything beyond letting the alcohol burn itself clean out of the system. It wasn't fair. The man had no right to remain sheltered from this.

Someone shrieked a breathy gasp. Gillian was on the patio, her profile outlining the two hands in front of her lips. "Oh, I'm sorry. You scared me," she said in a whisper, not wanting to wake Brent. As if it was so easy. "Are the kids sleeping?"

"For now." Alex walked onto the patio, glancing back at Brent to see if he would rustle. He remained motionless. Gillian flinched with the next blazing flash and Alex thought of holding her, of taking her hand or putting an arm around her shoulder. "Which way is that?" Alex pointed towards what seemed to be the source of the light. "West?"

"More like southwest. I thought it was lightning at first, but I don't hear a thing." She looked back. "What do you think it is?"

Hayden and Alex shook their heads, not saying a word in reply, weary from what was becoming the crushing burden of ignorance.

"I'm sorry about Brent," Gillian said, looking through the window. "He drank too much tonight. It's how he copes with stress."

No one replied, watching the ridge of trees, waiting for the next muted burst of light.

Gillian asked, "What do you two think you'll do tomorrow? Are you going to go on your way?"

"I'm not sure," Hayden said.

Alex answered, "I want to go see my mother and stepdad. They're out by Kootenay Lake. Not too far north from Spokane. At some point, we need to drive out there."

Gillian nodded and smiled. "I would love nothing more than to have Garrett and his family drive here. Just pull up in the morning and call out for us," Gillian started crying and apologized again. Alex pulled her closer but Gillian pushed her way out of the embrace. "No, I shouldn't be crying. We all need to be strong. We don't know what's happened. We need to be strong."

"Mom, Dad." Caleb was in the living room, rubbing his eyes. "What's going on?"

"Just go back to bed," Hayden said, hurrying inside.

"What's going on?"

"I think it's a storm," Alex answered, whispering. "It's just lightning. Now, let's get back to bed downstairs."

"But there's no thunder?"

"It's just really far away." Alex heard cries through the floor, a weak but prolonged whimper. "Was Sara up when you left?"

Caleb nodded. "She started crying. She's scared. That's why I came up."

"Shit," Alex hurried towards the stairs, Sara's weeping growing in volume with each step. The door to her room was open and a flash beamed out into the hallway. Sara was sitting up on the bed, calling for her mother in between hyperventilating gasps. Alex grabbed her and Sara grappled her arms and legs around.

"I'm sorry, I'm sorry." Alex said, not yet sure what she was apologizing for, "I'm here."

"What is that?" Sara asked, looking towards the window.

"Just a storm."

"Don't go, Mommy. Don't go."

"I'm not going anywhere. I'm staying here."

"Don't go, Mommy."

"I'm not going anywhere, Sara. I promise. I'm not going to leave you. I'm never going to leave you." Alex lay down, taking Sara with her, pulling the sheets over. Hayden entered the room with Caleb, ushering him back to his own bed. Hayden then hung a blanket from the blinds, securing the top with clothespins, assuring Caleb that it was just lightning, that these strange storms happen sometimes, that he wasn't going anywhere, that they would all sleep in the same room tonight. As Sara sniffled and Alex kissed her ringlets of hair, she whispered into Sara's ears, "I'm never going to leave you," repeating it like a mantra to soothe her own spirit.

Daylight crept beneath the blanket that Hayden had hung

the night before, a black and navy fleece adorned with the beaming portrait of Thomas the Train Engine. For a few seconds, Alex didn't think about where she was but instead felt Sara in the crook of her arm and stared at that eternally optimistic and telegenic locomotive. Hayden and Caleb were just out of reach on another bed, their breaths steady, a whistle in her son's inhalations. Alex was exhausted and closed her eyes again, rolling her face back towards Sara's hair. Then, in one moment, it all came back to her. In one moment, her listless eyes became eager and alert. Sara rolled over and Alex didn't want to rustle her. Her wonderful daughter was still in a dream, still insulated and safe from the terrifying world around her. She looked up towards the wavering space between that blanket and the window, able to discern nothing about the world outside other than that the sun was up. There wasn't a clock in the room. She heard the groaning creak of gentle footsteps upstairs, the gait of someone attempting to be as weightless as possible.

"Good morning," Brent said, his eyes and grin directed towards Sara, the girl's hair wild as if unspooled and impossible to put back into place. Alex had carried her up the steps, her back against one arm, knees draped over the other.

"Good morning," Alex noticed the mug in Brent's hand. She first wondered if there was liquor in that drink—a typical move of her father's—and then realized that he'd made coffee. That meant power, she figured. She looked around, trying to mute any excitement. "Is the electricity back on?"

Brent grimaced and shook his head. "I used a camping stove to boil the water. It's instant. There's enough water for more, if you want."

"Thanks." Alex strained to let down her daughter. "Here,

Sara, go look at the books on the couch. I'll get you something to eat." She then looked at Brent, expectant and apologetic. "Do you have any fruit, or something?"

"I want milk." Sara declared from across the room.

"I don't think they have any milk, honey. The fridge has no power. I'll get you something." She looked back to Brent, "I'm sorry. I feel like—"

"No, no. Don't apologize. I don't know what we'd do if you four weren't here. We don't have much, but take whatever you want. Please."

Alex thanked him, grabbed a leopard-skin banana from a fruit bowl and cut it into mushy slices. It wasn't until Alex ate a piece that she realized how hungry she was. She brought over the plate to Sara and decided to make herself some instant coffee. The very sight and feeling of a steaming mug in her hand lent this moment an air of normalcy that was both appreciated and fleeting. She asked Brent, "How are you feeling?"

"I'm okay."

She nodded, watching Sara, assuming she wasn't listening. "Did you sleep through the flashing last night?"

Brent grimaced, his very expression an attempt at an apology. He looked at Sara and then back to Alex, shaking his head. "I'm sorry. Had too much to drink last night. Think it was just the nerves. The whole day. I must have had a lot more than I realized. Gillian told me what happened, but I don't remember it. I'm sorry. I shouldn't have gotten so carried away. I should have been there for everyone."

Alex looked out from the living room window, the few clouds mere threads of stretched cotton. The spire points of the treetops didn't sway or rustle. It was yet another perfect summer morning. The 15th of August. She thought of assuring Brent that he shouldn't be the one apologizing, but instead Alex held onto that reply, not sure if she was ready to concede so easily. Remembering him on that chair, his chin buried into the fat of his neck while the world outside exploded all around them, it wasn't fair. He drank himself through the nightmare. But right now, Alex needed him. There was every chance that she would be dead if Brent and Gillian hadn't invited them over. "Don't be sorry for anything," she said. "I think we're all still in a daze."

"You guys know what you'll be doing today?"

Alex shook her head. "You?"

The Captain had a plan and he explained it to Alex with step-by-step instructions, a teacher to his class of one. He and Hayden would drive to Maple Falls, the nearest town, a crossroads in the forest with little more than a general store and a church. They would leave as soon as Hayden was awake and take Brent's truck. He described it as an information gathering expedition, seeking other survivors and their knowledge. He assured that they would be gone for no more than an hour. He would never leave the women and children alone at a time like this for even a second more than was absolutely necessary. When Alex made a joke about looting a store, Brent glared back stoic, disapproving of her sense of humor. He was going into details of distances and directions when Hayden emerged from the stairs, Caleb a pair of steps behind. "You up for a little adventure? Get to the bottom of this?" Brent said to Hayden. The men would venture forth into the wilderness. Hayden was in complete agreement, saying that he'd been thinking the same thing. Alex wanted to pull him aside and remind him that they could leave. They could start their journey to Kootenay Lake.

But for the men, time was of the essence. Hayden advised that they should depart immediately. "It just makes sense," Hayden assured Alex with a paternal kiss to her forehead. Minutes later, they were gone. Caleb wanted to play outside and explore the forest, but Alex demanded that he stay indoors. She needed her kids to remain as close to her as possible, angry that Hayden left without any discussion. It wasn't that Brent's plan was unreasonable or foolhardy—it was the lack of debate. It was decreed. They were gone. Once again, she was left alone with the children. She might as well have been instructed to gather berries in hand-woven baskets. As the cool, brisk morning shadows withered away beneath the looming, scorching sun, Caleb intensified his pestering about going into the forest, promising that he would stay close, but Alex couldn't allow it. Outside, anything could happen. "Maybe when Dad gets back," she said. He whined and she wanted to remind him that this wasn't a fucking holiday.

Gillian looked towards her and chuckled. "Oh, boys. Right?"

Brent and Hayden returned with supplies that filled the back of the pickup. Caleb and Sara ran towards their father and hugged him as if he'd been on expedition for days. Brent walked right past Alex, keeping his eyes on the ground a few feet ahead of his steps while carrying twenty-pound propane tanks, one in each arm. Alex asked if they found anyone and Hayden shook his head with terse pivots, lips tight. Just his expression made her heart race. While they were gone—while the kids played in the living room, while they complained of being bored, while they built a fort out of sofa cushions and chairs, while they rattled the keys on the piano—Alex could be tricked into thinking that Hayden would return with news, good news, information that would wake everyone up from their collective nightmare. She delved into outlandish hypothetical scenarios: that the men would find military personnel rounding up survivors, bringing them to secure safe zones, assuring everyone that the worst was now over. Things were about to get better. Lines of communication were being re-networked. What happened wasn't as dire as first thought. Whatever it was. But Hayden didn't want to relay what he'd seen, just that they needed assistance with transporting provisions. There were boxes of canned goods, deep plastic crates with produce— tomatoes, peppers, apples, bananas, green leaf lettuce, onions, potatoes—and plastic wrapped flats of water, one after the next. There were paper bags filled with chocolate bars, bags of chips, gummy candies. Alex tried to ask Hayden what happened and he told her to wait. He then gave her a warm beer, ripped out from a box of twenty-four, and asked Gillian and Brent to watch the kids so that they could talk out by their car.

Hayden cracked open his can and strained to take more than an abbreviated gulp before requiring another breath. "What happened?" she asked. "Where the fuck did you get all that stuff from? I thought Brent was above that sort of thing? Did you find anyone else?"

He looked at Alex, caught by the wording of her last question. She didn't want to repeat herself and instead let him take his time. He then said: "They are all," he shook his head, his eyes weary, just now willing to give in to a few tears that waded at the rims of each eyelid, "in the river." He swallowed and took another sip of beer. "The Nooksack River. Never even heard of it until Brent told me its name. The Nooksack." Hayden elongated each syllable, as if about to make a joke. He took another gulp.

"Hayden, what did you see?"

"We didn't find anyone. We knocked on a few houses and no one answered. But their doors were open. Wide open. When we drove to town, we saw a car that went off the road into the river. An old 90's Civic hatchback. I don't know why we didn't stop then. We just drove past. We drove to Maple Falls and there was no one around." He looked at the beer in his hand, the aluminum can quivering within his boney fingers. "The store in town was left unlocked without anyone inside. The place was untouched. Nothing out of place or knocked over. We just went in and took what we wanted. Didn't even have to rationalize with each other. Didn't say a word to each other. We just started taking stuff. We were hardly in there for more than a few minutes before knowing we had to get out. So, we got out. We drove back here and that's when we saw that Civic again. Back where the highway comes up to the river. The car was down, like this." He formed a sharp angle with the palms of both hands. "We stepped out and saw that the driver was still in there, crushed between the steering wheel and seat. But then we saw the river. There were other cars. And there were people, bodies washed up on the shore. We saw dozens of them face down in the water, caught on banks and logjams. Fucking dozens of them."

"Hayden, I'm sorry—"

He looked at Alex, his eyes inches from hers. "No, I don't think you get it. It's not just the bodies. It's that we drove that stretch of highway yesterday morning on our way here. It's like, not even five kilometers away. None of that was there then. Whatever happened to those people, whatever made them do that, it happened while we were here, right here, with our kids.

While we sat on that deck and drank scotch, people walked into the Nooksack. Fucking, right there—" Hayden pointed down the gravel driveway, through a dense mass of trees, "Just a five-minute drive away. Part of me wants to get us all packed into the car and get the fuck out of here right now. Part of me thinks we should stay put. I don't know. I have no idea. That's the most terrifying part. I don't have a fucking clue."

Gillian broke down in the middle of the afternoon, sobbing to herself, telling anyone who approached her to stay away with a tone that implied profanity. Sara asked why the woman was crying and Alex told her that she was tired. It seemed to quell Sara's curiosity. Hayden took Caleb outside, promising Alex that they'd not stray far. Brent moved on from warm beer to whiskey, cracking the foil off from the cap of a half-gallon bottle procured from the Maple Falls general store before taking his designated spot in the Captain's Chair, overlooking the motionless forest and hazy blue skies in behind. Sara asked to go outside, to play with Caleb, but Alex wouldn't let her. She had to stay inside. There was no tantrum too intense to make Alex relent. Her three-year-old daughter would not go outside. Not yet. There were bodies clogging the river just a few kilometers away. Alex couldn't even recall the name of the river, the one that Hayden kept repeating. She sat out on the balcony, content to weather Sara's pouting, watching Hayden and Caleb down below in the woods. When she looked through the windows towards Brent, he stared at the lifeless television set, his eyes locked and stern as if watching football amidst a crowd of ambivalent spectators. Sara started crying again and Brent glanced towards her, annoyed. He was trying to watch something, after all. Alex wanted to leave. She wanted to put everyone in the car and start driving. Right now, they were all waiting, but no one knew what for, exactly. Sara threw a block of Duplo, hitting her mother in the shoulder. Alex lunged up, surprising herself with how ready she was to hit her child. What would it matter at this point? What would a smack across the cheek mean in comparison to what was happening all around them? Sara looked at her mother, whined, and threw another block. That was it. Alex hit her, slapped her across the face and Sara went silent. For a second, she didn't make a noise. For a second, Alex thought that it was worthwhile. But she knew what would come next, and before Alex could think of what to say, Sara erupted, hiding her face, her eyes, trying to disappear. Alex thought of slapping her again. None of the rules of middle-class parenting mattered anymore. Just fucking shut up for one minute. You're alive, don't you realize that? Can't you appreciate that for just one fucking minute?

Alex picked her up, expecting Sara to push her away but instead she melted into her arms. "I'm sorry," Alex said in between shushing, bouncing her up and down like when she was a baby. Sara grappled in, crying, her snotty nose buried in to Alex's shoulder. "I'm sorry," she repeated, kissing her, looking out over the railing towards the forest where Hayden and Caleb were. "I'm sorry. Mommy's just tired." She looked around, expecting to see the figures of her husband and son any second. It was too early to think anything more than that. It had only been a few seconds.

They were gone.

Resisting the urge to call out, Alex walked the perimeter of the deck, trying to remain nonchalant. She assumed that Brent was still watching her. It had only been a few seconds. Maybe thirty. Maybe a minute. It was too early to panic. But she wanted to panic. It was too early to shout. She would appear frenzied and weak, like Gillian. But why the fuck did she care what Brent thought? She just hit her daughter—Brent's opinion was of no importance. She called out: "Hayden! Caleb!"

There was no reply.

They were gone.

She called out again, not wanting her tone to become hysterical. She was just calling out, curious. Brent opened the French doors, hardly staggering considering he must have been on his fifth drink, and asked what was wrong. Alex shook her head. She didn't want to be frantic. Sara looked at her, still sniffling, cheeks glistening from tears. "I don't know where Hayden and Caleb went. They were just down there, just a minute ago."

"What were they doing?"

"Just playing. Hayden? Caleb?"

Brent leaned so far over the railing that the heels of his slippers came off from the wood. Alex resisted yelling again, thinking about Sara.

"Alex." Hayden said from inside. He stood at the top of the stairs, Caleb a step behind him. "What's going on?"

She asked where he'd been and he told her that they just came around to the front door. It couldn't have been any more than a minute. Alex tried to laugh but instead tears rolled down one cheek and then the other. Brent patted her on the shoulder and walked back inside. Hayden came closer, his eyes telling her that he was scared with how fragile she was, that she should sit down, that she should get some rest.

The many old clocks around the house showed that it was eight in the evening. Gillian had yet to leave her bedroom and

Brent didn't seem bothered by the darkness that was filling their home. Hayden lit candles and Alex sat on the deck with a blanket wrapped around her, watching the sky. A cool breeze rustled the tops of the trees as the sun descended. Hayden put the kids to bed and Alex stayed on the chair, waiting. She noticed one star; she noticed a dozen.

When the first flash of light illuminated the valley, Alex flinched. She'd forgotten the intensity of it. A ferocious coruscation. But nothing else. No shuddering. No sound. Her stomach wound slowly, expecting the next strobe. She told herself she wasn't going to cry. She'd already broken down in front of everyone and now she would remain stoic, removed. The light burst across the sky and vanished. A sense of dread returned, not so much tapping her on the shoulders as it did grab her by the waist. This was that feeling of being told a diagnosis, an awful diagnosis that you've been casting aside thoughts of for weeks, for months. The creaking of the door preluded Hayden's entry on the deck. "Hey," he said, unsure what else there was to add.

"Where's Caleb and Sara?" Alex asked in a croak.

"They're downstairs, playing. They're tired but not asleep."

"Shit," Alex said, shaking her head. "He's going to be up here any second now."

"It's not like we can hide this from them."

"How long can we keep telling them that we don't know what's going on?" She had to pause for a moment. She sat up, breathed in and then out. She wasn't going to weep. "We're supposed to have the answers."

"We're not *supposed* to do anything."

Alex said, "I feel like we're not supposed to be seeing this. I feel like we're supposed to be dead right now."

"Dad?" Caleb's voice cracked as he approached the door. "It's happening again?"

Hayden said to Alex, "I got this," and turned towards the open doors. "Caleb, go back downstairs. Watch Sara."

Caleb waited, inspecting the forest and surrounding mountains as they'd blaze into existence and then vanish all in the snap of a finger.

"Caleb," Hayden repeated, his tone harsh, "Go now. Don't leave Sara alone. She needs you with her. Go." Caleb listened, backing up slowly before running between the candlelit tables towards the stairs.

"Sara's going to be up here in a minute," Alex said with a sigh.

"We should go down with them," Hayden turned, ready to go inside.

"Don't go yet, please." Alex reached out for Hayden's hand and pulled him in closer, waited for the next burst of light before continuing. "You said that you and Brent saw all those people in the river. Then, why do you think we're still here? Why do you think we're alive?"

Hayden squeezed her hand, struggling to find an answer. "Luck of the draw?"

Alex chuckled as if to substitute for a profanity. "I don't feel lucky."

"Because it's not luck. It's probability." He sighed. "Give enough people a hundred coins, and eventually someone will come up with all heads. I think we're that someone."

"What's the jackpot, then?"

Hayden shook his head, either unsure of the answer or unwilling to divulge. "We should go downstairs."

*　　*　　*

When the last candle on the night table flickered out, Alex could still hear the unintelligible argument between Brent and Gillian. It began as a conversation while Sara was still up, civil to the point of banal. Alex kissed her daughter's wispy, tangled hair while retelling her rendition of *Olivia* from memory, eliciting reluctant giggles. But now Sara slept and Brent's baritone voice enunciated slow and steady, replying with two or three word sentences to Gillian's fluttering questions and statements. Peering up towards the Thomas blanket, Alex watched the flashes of light illuminate its furry tips and wrinkled edges. She couldn't see across the room, couldn't tell if Hayden was awake. There was no point keeping her eyes open. She was tired—she didn't think she'd ever before been this exhausted, not even in those weeks after Sara's birth—but she couldn't sleep. She couldn't hear the rhythms of Caleb's or Hayden's breaths through the argument. She didn't know the time and couldn't see a clock. And then the voices would calm; Brent and Gillian stopped talking and resumed moments later with mumbled whispers. She'd kiss Sara in the nape of her neck and the girl mumbled a polysyllabic moan. Alex had to keep her thoughts contained to this room, to her family that was together and safe. They were alive. They were lucky. She gripped Sara's shoulder and wished for sleep. She would awake in the morning and it would be another perfect summer's day. And there would be no power. And there would be no other signs of life. And there would be a log jam of human corpses just down the road, not even five kilometers away, in that river whose name she still could not recall.

Brent yelled and Gillian shrieked. Alex jutted up, unsure if she'd been awoken. Heavy footsteps rattled the wooden beams and Alex whispered out to Hayden. He had not been sleeping. Alex knew what she wanted to say but was reluctant to come across as rash or hysterical. She didn't utter a word, waiting for the flashing light outside to mark the passage of time. She then whispered: "We should go."

"When?"

"Now."

"What?"

Alex slipped her arms out from Sara and crawled down onto the carpet, urging Hayden to do the same. They sat beside each other with their backs against the bedroom door, facing the window. A crisp white rectangle traced the crinkled lines and drooping corners of the blanket every nineteen seconds. "We need to get out of here. If not now, then first thing in the morning before Brent and Gillian wake up. We need to get into our car and drive."

"I don't know," Hayden shook his head. "When I saw the river. And all that. I don't know if we should be in a rush to drive anywhere. We're safe here."

Alex looked up to the featureless ceiling. Gillian was crying. "Are we? We're just wasting time. Gillian won't want us to leave. And Brent. Brent, I don't trust him. He's a drunk. He's unpredictable."

"We'd probably be dead if we hadn't met those two."

She didn't expect such blunt words so close to the children. She struggled with a reply.

He added: "It's true. You know it. We'd probably be in the river with the rest of them."

She'd visualized their SUV lodged in the rushing rapids, Sara and Caleb in the back, underwater, eyes wide open and hair wriggling weightless. It was impossible to hold back the tears and she was angry at Hayden for saying such a thing. It seemed cheap. "It doesn't matter. That doesn't matter now. Going forward, we need to get moving. Pack the car once Brent and Gillian are asleep. Wake up the kids at the first light of morning and drive."

"Drive where?"

"To Barbara and Kevin's."

"And how?"

Alex didn't understand Hayden's question. She was slow to answer, unable to keep herself from saying the words with a patronizing clarity. "By driving on the road."

"We don't know what's happened. We don't know if the highways are clear. We don't know if the roads are safe."

"So, what? We'll just stay here for the rest of our lives?"

"There's a big difference between the rest of our lives and a few more days."

"You never fucking trust me."

"Don't go there. You didn't see what I saw in the river there. You didn't fucking see that."

Alex wished that she could tell if Caleb and Sara were listening. She leaned in close to his ear: "If it wasn't for me, you'd be dead. You talk about it being luck that we're alive. Well, fuck that. It's because of me. Back home, you thought I was crazy, but I'm the reason we made it out and you can't deny it. I'm the one who got you. I'm the one. So, give me credit for once and trust me when I say that we need to go."

Hayden sighed. Alex wanted to hit him. He said, "We don't *need* to go just yet."

"Fine. But I *want* to go. Give me this, Hayden. Give me this."

*   *   *

Once Hayden agreed, Alex didn't dare sleep, his consent feeling tenuous. If she slept, she might not awaken until after Brent and Gillian. Then they'd be trapped for another languid day. Although Hayden lay on the floor at the foot of Caleb's bed, Alex kept her back against the door. It could have been midnight. It could have been five in the morning. She'd close her eyes and think of stupid things, happy to have a moment to think of stupid things—like the vegetables growing in the back garden of their house, how they hadn't been watered and would be wilting in the afternoon heat. It had been days since she left their house, their garden, the shriveling tomato plants. She saw Sara, her face begging for permission to tread upon the soil in her bare feet. The grass surrounding the garden beds hadn't been cut in over a week and the tops of the blades wrapped around the girl's toes. Alex told Sara that it was alright—she could take a couple of the tomatoes right off the vine—but to not step into the dirt. Because then Alex would have to carry her inside straight to the bathtub. That would be a problem. And Alex walked through her house, holding Sara, hearing the television. It was just a dream, she would think, relieved to know that it was just a dream. "Of course, this is a dream," Alex said to Sara. "Of course." It didn't make sense. She hugged her daughter and looked out the window to the towers and planes and traffic of the city. Her hands gripped the edge of the countertop. The piercing tip of the sturdy and inflexible chef's knife was spotless, just out of reach.

Hayden's placid grip woke up Alex, her eyes blinking open to the daylight of the room, to Caleb sitting on the bed and Hayden standing over her. There was no worse feeling. For that moment—the moment she realized that this was her reality, the cool, dark basement bedroom in the morning, her children rubbing their eyes, blankets still covering their legs, anxious faces tracing the movements of their parents without saying a word—Alex thought that she would rather be dead, unthinking. A corpse in the river.

"It's time to go," Hayden said.

Alex stood up. She carried Sara, the girl's knees against Alex's waist and head jostling above her shoulder. Alex looked up the stairs towards the living room, hearing nothing and seeing no one. She laid a note on the steps as Hayden eased open the front door. He'd already taken supplies from the kitchen, items that he'd looted from the general store, and placed them in bulging bags that rested against their SUV's tires. Apples, bananas, a loaf of bread, peanut butter, packs of instant noodles and one-liter cartons of from-concentrate juice. Alex felt struck by the bracing freshness of the air outside; the bedroom in which they'd spent the night was stuffy, the smoke from expired candles still hanging in the air. There was not a cloud in the sky and the tall stalks of trees stood firm and still. The sun had yet to burst above the peaks of the surrounding mountains, lighting the mossy yard and parked cars without definition, shadows somehow pale. Caleb started asking a question—all he got out were the words "*What are*"—but both Hayden and Alex shushed him at the same time, ordering him to be quiet, that they would say more later on. First it was into the SUV. Without asking, Hayden took the driver's seat while Alex clipped in Sara. She then sat beside her husband and stared towards the A-frame house, watching it wobble and slink away as Hayden reversed. She lowered the window and relished in more of the crisp air, feeling sorry for Gillian. It was not fair to her to be left alone with a useless alcoholic. Hayden turned and the house swung out of view, replaced with a blur of shadowy tree trunks and then the gravel driveway. Rocks clattered against the undercarriage as Hayden accelerated and Alex reminded herself that none of this was fair. Just luck of the draw.

Hayden veered onto the highway, back towards Maple Falls. There were only two reasonable routes east through the Cascade Mountains: through Canada or through Washington State. Aside from the details of an erroneously refolded roadmap, neither of them knew the American route, so they drove back along the same narrow highway that they came in on, back to the northern border.

They passed the Honda Civic that Hayden referenced the day before, its hind wheels up in the air, its hood shy of the tumbling current. Glimpses of the river were only offered in flashes between stands of trees, mere flashes of color in the sandy gray and gravel river. Hayden told Caleb that they might see some strange things on their journey but it was his job to listen, it was his job to help Sara. Caleb conceded without any further convincing. Alex turned the radio to AM, the speakers crackling with static, and spun the tuner all the way to the left before twisting the knob click-by-click, Khz-by-Khz. Alex shushed upon thinking she'd heard speech, adjusting the volume and directing an ear towards one of the speakers. But there was only a pop and hiss, never a voice, never a melody. She switched to FM and systematically turned the dial. When the display read 108 Mhz and budged no further, she punched the knob to turn off the radio.

"Try again in a few minutes. It can't hurt," Hayden said. Alex replied with a limp nod. Bursts of sunlight shimmered above the treetops and into the rearview mirrors. The time on the display read 6:12 in the morning. Without anything to do,

Alex yearned for a coffee. It seemed so trivial and selfish to think about, but she figured that a cup would help. Make it feel like this was just any other road trip with the kids in the backseat, still too tired to cause trouble, the cool mountain air running between her fingers. They drove through a small town, a hamlet of just a few streets and a gas station. The leaves of elegant deciduous trees were turning amber, a reflection of the long, hot summer as opposed to the distant start of autumn. The idle citizens of this village were still asleep at this young hour of the morning. There wasn't any traffic and the family was making good time.

The forest to their right receded and revealed sprawling grassland with grazing horses that ignored their passing vehicle. Alex counted at least four large homes, each with separate two or three-car garages. She asked if they should drive up one of the driveways to check for people, but Hayden shook his head. Making sure that Caleb couldn't hear, he directed Alex towards the grandiose houses with a twitch of his chin. "Look at the doors. None of them are closed. We don't know what we'll find around there. We should just drive." He was right. Every front door was wide open, a strange and incongruous detail amongst the surrounding tranquility. The dense forest then returned, enclosing both sides of the highway. As the undulating highway departed the foothills of Mount Baker, these forests gave way to farmland, rows of tall cornfields, a dense green plain that stretched west and north to reveal the extent of the Fraser River valley and the mountains that hemmed in the region. Houses lined either side of the road every few hundred meters, trucks and cars parked in driveways. They were in the town of Sumas with concrete sidewalks between the pavement and the gravel shoulder, stout and humble bungalows surrounded by wooden fences. Stop signs, playground zones and a local school. Churches, family restaurants, stores, a notice for the Canadian border at the next right.

"Pull over," Alex said as they approached the intersection. He slowed onto the gravel and stopped the car. Alex's heart was racing and it seemed ridiculous to react this way. She searched around for anything, knowing that if she saw anyone— a single survivor—then she would feel so much better. Her body could unwind. They would not be the only ones. It was not a mistake to leave. Hayden surveyed the area, perhaps thinking the same thing. Perhaps his heart was racing, as well. To Alex, it didn't seem possible for him to be so truly calm.

"Why are we stopping?" Caleb asked. Hayden looked to Alex. It was her job to answer.

"Dad and I are just thinking."

"But you're not talking," Caleb said.

"We're thinking, I said. We don't need to talk to be thinking, do we?" She looked back to Hayden. The engine idled and they looked around, as if waiting for someone.

Hayden said: "It was your idea to go."

"I know. I know." Alex leaned out the window, breathing in, the air a tonic, listening for anything. A crow cawed from the top of a wooden electric pole before taking off into flight.

"Okay." Alex nodded. "Go."

The car turned and accelerated, the road a two-lane line of longitude. Alex turned the radio back on to conduct another search of the airwaves, this time an impatient scan, never lingering at any specific frequency, her eyes up towards the road and surrounding landscape. The Canadian border was one mile away. Empty cars were parked on the side of the road, doors left open into adjacent lanes revealing abandoned bags and jackets left on the seats. A single high-heel shoe strewn in the middle of the lane shuddered the SUV as Hayden drove over it. The Canadian border was half a mile away. Digital displays with estimated wait times remained dormant. The road split into almost a dozen lanes for the hundreds of waiting cars that were nowhere to be seen. Signs informed passengers to have their identification ready. Empty glass booths for border guards separated each lane beneath the tall canopy. Most of the checkpoints were closed, the red and white striped arms horizontal. Only three were up. Hayden guided the vehicle over speed bumps, looking around for anyone. There was no one. Welcome to British Columbia, read the cheerful billboard with pastel sunny yellows, tranquil ocean blues. Signs reminded motorists to think in metric. The rural landscape had been swapped for a suburban one, bold arrows directing buyers towards new subdivisions with two-car garages, stainless steel appliances, private backyards and that contented, familial bliss that only comes with a new home from a trusted builder. Highway One was two kilometers away. They passed strip malls, cars parked in rows and columns. Alex stopped searching the radio and Hayden slowed the SUV as they approached the exit. He looked at her. "Maybe we should try going back home?"

Alex had thought the same thing. Their house should only have been a forty-five-minute drive west. She leaned her head out the window again, tempted to open the door and stand out in the middle of the road. "I don't know." She then sniffed. "Do you smell that?"

"It's all the farmland."

Alex shook her head. "No, it's not that. It's different."

Hayden breathed in, shaking his head, about to disagree.

His head stopped and he inhaled again. He seemed reluctant to reply.

Alex directed him ahead with a twitch of her chin. "I think there's a strip mall up ahead. A Walmart and stuff. Let's drive up there. See if there's anyone."

Hayden nodded and moved ahead with caution, scanning east and west as they drove over the empty highway, the lone artery that connected the entirety of the country from east to west. A subtle but distinctly acidic scent in the air became heavy, something pickled, a wafting ammonia. The road ahead was packed with motionless cars, some strewn along the sides of the road, others in orderly lanes. Hayden stopped, still too distant to make out anything in detail. Crows swirled over the idle vehicles like fruit flies. "There's no way we can get through that," he said and waited for Alex to reply. She stared. Her chest quivered. She looked at the bandage on her left finger, her breaths short but feeling entirely lucid. "Screw this," Hayden muttered and backed up to turn the car around. Alex nodded as if agreeing to what Hayden had said and he took a hard left to enter the exit lane, merging onto the vacant six-lane highway and headed east. He lowered the windows and the rattling, ruffling breeze flushed out the stench. Alex looked back, unable to see anything besides the weathered and cracked pavement. Hayden accelerated until the engine whirred, taking gentle turns by straddling two lanes, hurtling down the highway as fast as their vehicle would allow.

Alex leaned over, trying to keep her voice buried beneath the wail of the engine: "What if we come across something like that up ahead?"

"What was that?" Caleb asked.

Both Alex and Hayden pretended not to hear their son.

Alex repeated, "Hayden, what do—"

"I don't know," he said, ending it there. The engine whined, the needle now jostling up against the 180 km/h notch. Alex wanted him to slow down. "We don't need to be going this fast."

"We need to get the fuck out of here."

Caleb repeated: "What was that?"

"You need to stop asking questions right now," Alex chided, her eyes not lingering on either child when turning back, instead resuming her focus on the road, the dashed white lines blurring beneath their hood. The mountains shuffled to the side as the highway curved and revealed the morning sun, glaring golden into her eyes. She flipped down the visor, wincing to look at the distant details on the highway ahead. There seemed to be something. "Hayden—"

"I know." He'd taken his foot off from the accelerator. The howling engine unwound. There were cars on the highway ahead, but the road was so flat that it was impossible to determine just how many from so far away. Hayden eased the brakes. Through the open windows, Alex could once again detect that smell. It was rotting meat.

"Just stop the car," Alex said and Hayden obeyed, everyone jostling forward into their seatbelts. A conspicuous hill, forested with vibrant shades of green coniferous trees, descended down to the flat valley floor where it met the highway ahead. Motionless vehicles clogged the eastbound lanes and ditch. A tight wire barrier separated the two sides of the highway but several cars had broken through, spilling onto the opposing but otherwise clear lanes.

"Come out with me," Alex said to Hayden and he agreed. He assured Caleb and Sara that they were going to stay close to the car then closed the windows and shut the doors. The cluster of vehicles couldn't have been more than another half-kilometer away. The smell was unavoidable, accosting them in wafts. Hayden stood on one of the cylindrical posts holding the wire barricade, granting him another couple of feet of height.

Alex asked, "How many cars are there?"

"Lots."

"Can you see anyone? Any," Alex didn't want to say the word *bodies* and thankfully she didn't have to. Hayden shook his head. She looked back to the children and smiled. She then turned so that her expression and lips were hidden to both. "What the fuck are we going to do?"

"We're going to have to go through that."

"You see room to drive?"

Hayden shook his head. He waited, hoping that Alex would figure it out herself. "We have to walk through there."

"With Sara and Caleb? And just leave the car?"

"I don't think there's another option. If we walk on the westbound lanes we can bypass most of it."

"And then what?"

Hayden sighed. "You think I want to do this?"

"And then what?"

"Get into another car? Hope that we can find one with keys that are still in the ignition? I can go ahead and check." Hayden nodded to himself, taking a deep breath. "I'll make sure that it's possible. I'll get a car ready for us and then we can all go together. I'll carry Caleb, you carry Sara."

"But—"

"There's no other way." He appeared nervous about wasting any time, "Go back to the car. I'll run up ahead. If there's anything wrong—anything—I'll come right back. But I don't like standing around here in the middle of this highway. I feel," he searched for a word, shaking his head while looking towards the mountains to the north and south. "Like we're on display here. Like we're being watched. I'm going."

Hayden had already taken a few steps backwards towards the assembly of vehicles, nodding, assuring Alex that there was nothing else to do. He then spun and jogged ahead. "Okay," Alex said to herself before facing the kids, smiling in a way that she figured must have appeared disingenuous to even children of their age. She opened the door and Caleb was already in the process of asking where Dad had gone. "He's going to check on a few things. The road is blocked and we're maybe going to have to get into a different car. Daddy's just making sure that everything is okay up there," Alex looked up the highway. Hayden was now a small figure against the quivering blacktop. Soon he would jump over the barrier, soon he would move beside the wreckage, soon he would be out of sight. Caleb asked about leaving the car and Alex shushed him, her eyes forward. Hayden stopped jogging, stopped moving. He looked back and Alex couldn't tell if he was signaling her. Caleb asked if Dad was going to be all right and Alex assured him that he knew what he was doing. "Trust me. We're going to be fine." Alex wished that she found a different way to assuage her son's concerns. He surely knew that she was lying. Hayden climbed over the barrier and moved across from the vehicles. Seconds later, he was out of sight. She was on her own with the kids in the middle of a desolate highway. She leaned forward and winced, aware of her thudding heartbeat, hearing every breath, wondering if her children could perceive them, if Caleb might see the bulging pulse in her neck. She turned on the radio, her eyes fixated on the road ahead while her right hand spun the tuner, appreciating the static that now filled the stuffy interior. Hayden was still nowhere to be seen and Alex wished that she had started counting instead of turning on the radio. Sara asked for her and Alex reached back to hold her hands. "I'm right here. I'm not going anywhere. I'm right here." What if Hayden didn't come back? She didn't want to ask herself this question, but it tumbled out from her thoughts as clear as if prompted by someone else. Nothing was happening. She remembered the radio and continued with the tuner. "Come on," Alex said to herself, no longer worried about anyone else hearing her. "Come on." When would she go out to check? Would she take the kids with her? Or would she turn around and drive? "Hayden, come on," Alex said to the dash, like he was right there, just within earshot. It felt good to say this, to let her kids hear. "Come—"

A person ran towards her on the westbound lanes. It was Hayden and he was sprinting, his previous trepidation now a nervous urgency. She waved and hoped that he would do something in reply. "Here's Daddy," Alex said in her best attempt at being calm, letting go of Sara's hand and stepping out from the car as his steps slowed. She closed the door behind her. She asked, "It's okay?"

Hayden stopped, breaths wheezing. He didn't shake his head or nod. He looked at Alex with eyes that widened. "I got a car that starts. A white Golf. It will work. We need to go." He seemed ready to open the door to get Caleb out.

"Hayden," Alex grabbed his arm. "What is over there?"

He didn't want to talk about it. He didn't have to say a word. He shook his head, eyes glazed.

"Okay." Alex said. "What should I do?"

"Just get the bare essentials from the car. Water, what food we can carry with Caleb and Sara in our arms. We're going to have to leave a lot behind. We're going to do this in one trip. Once we get over there, we get in the car and go. There will be no going back."

"Okay."

Alex felt diminutive but gratefully so, not yet wanting to know the details of what he'd seen and yet aware that these were the final moments of her ignorance. She opened the back of the SUV as Hayden let out Caleb, kneeling down to instruct his son eye-to-eye: "Okay, so listen, Caleb. I'm going to run with you and Mom is going to take Sara. There are some things over there that you don't want to see, okay? So, when I tell you to, you close your eyes. And I mean you close your eyes. When we get to the new car, you're going to see some things. Some bad things. You'll have to remain as calm as you possibly can, okay? I need this from you so that Sara doesn't get too upset. She's not as old as you and she's going to be scared, okay? It's going to be hard, but you're going to have to stay calm and listen. Just make sure you listen and do what we say. Okay?"

Caleb was trying to conceal his tears, wiping them back with the backs of his wrists, nodding, saying, "Okay," when necessary. Hayden looked up to Alex, knowing that she had heard everything he said and swallowed.

Alex carried three plastic bags with food and water over one shoulder while supporting Sara with her other arm. Hayden led the way a few steps ahead in the opposing lane, his pace sturdy and rhythmic, Caleb holding tight onto his father's right hand, head down, watching his feet. Their three sets of steps clattered against the asphalt and into the expansive surroundings. Right then, there were no other sounds. Just scraping, skittering soles upon the asphalt. Sara's quivering breaths, Caleb's sniffles. The mass of automobiles had pressed up against the wire barrier before having broken through, concealing the extent of the obstruction. Cars were strewn and crumpled, on their sides and on their roofs, seams of grey and white piercing through the colorful coatings. The sour, sharp smell of rotting meat grew in bursts with each gust of wind. Old, uncooked chicken bones left in the bottom of the garbage for weeks. Hayden pulled Caleb in closer, telling him to close his eyes. Sara looked up and Alex's tone was one of scolding: "Keep your head down." A dusty-black compact was crushed like a beer can, the hood compressed and facing the adjacent lane, its windshield shattered and twinkling against the pavement. A pair of crows glided overhead and landed on the hood of a delivery van, their talons scratching against the metal, eyes like black stones plucked from a river, watching these scrambling intruders. That was where Alex saw the first body. She looked away but then back—tufts of gray hair sprung from the head of a person facedown into the steering wheel. "Keep your head down," she said to Sara. Cars had broken through the barrier and she spotted more figures against the windows, back in their seats, thrust through the windshield and onto the hoods. *Figures*, she thought, not people. People move, people look. These were solid, static, like mannequins. Flies buzzed past her face and Alex didn't have a free hand to swat them away. She wanted to remain focused on this, on these insects that glided past her eyes and lips. She'd rather cringe from the swarm of flies than from the figures in their cars. But then she saw a child, a girl in the backseat of a sedan with straight black hair obscuring the pale skin of her face, eyes open, not older than five, her skin dotted with flinching pests. "Keep your head down," she kept repeating to Sara, not certain if her daughter was looking. Hurrying around the obstruction, the westbound lanes cleared but something changed. The cars ahead appeared to have been parked, arranged in a deliberate array. And they were smeared with blood, now rusty and chestnut. The bodies were no longer inside the vehicles but on the asphalt, faces bloated and ruptured, mouths open in a frozen scream. These weren't figures. These were the corpses of human beings, torn apart, ripped open, strewn like litter between vehicles. Here, the flies were dense, their collective whine rising above the scratching of panicked footsteps. They scattered on Alex's cheeks and lips and in her mouth as she told Caleb to keep his head down, to watch his feet. Crows cawed, the sharp tips of their beaks following the family's stride, telling them to move on. This is no place for beings like you.

"Hayden!" Alex yelled, "How much farther?"

"Just follow me."

Some of the victims were so dismembered that they no longer resembled human beings. They were cuts of meat. When all Alex saw was bone, blood and muscle, she wasn't as repulsed. These were carcasses, unidentifiable roadkill. Her eyes wouldn't linger on any one detail. It was when she saw the undeniable fragments of modern life—frozen in time but scarred by perverse details—that she thought she might throw up. A woman in her fluttering nylon coat and faded jeans, still wearing oversized sunglasses but with a twisted neck, face gawking towards her shoulder blades. A girl with sandy blonde hair wearing camouflage pants and a cream knit vest with russet holes the size of fists where there should have been eyes. Someone in a Starbucks uniform—the green apron still tied around the waist—with arms out to the side, fingers flayed, and skull crushed down to the thickness of his or her neck. Alex could not discern a gender. It kept going, these cars and trucks that had long ago come to a halt, their chassis intact, and yet enveloped by massacre. Caleb was staring at everything and Alex didn't have the voice to tell him to look away. An ashen haired lady with yellowed skin was pressed against the bumper of a delivery van, mouth torn apart.

"Hayden!"

"Up here," he said with an assuring tone. Lines of crows thrust up their shoulders and bellowed at the scampering family, their talons clattering against the pristine hoods of trucks. Alex pressed Sara's head into her shoulder and looked straight ahead. She had no right to witness the undignified end to so many lives. Caleb tripped but was kept from tumbling by Hayden's unrelenting grip, and for a moment her son was dragged with the tips of his shoes skittering against the asphalt. Hayden didn't say a word, pulling Caleb back up and carrying on. Alex could see a single vehicle ahead of all the others, a white compact car that looked to be splashed with mud, all four of its doors open, wings of a beetle ready for flight. Exhaust trickled out from the rear, twirling, vanishing. Looking to her right, the vehicles were once again scattered along the shoulder and ditch, pressed up into the barrier, crumbled and jagged. There was smoke in the air that cut through the fermented rot, an acrid exhaust that stuck onto the back of Alex's throat. Hayden carried Caleb over onto the eastbound lanes. They were seconds away from the Golf. Alex whispered into her daughter's ear, "Almost there, Sara. Almost there." There were bodies on the ground but Alex kept her eyes towards the open road and that one idling Volkswagen. Right leg over, left leg over, she crossed onto the other side of the highway. Hayden told Caleb to get in. The exhaust from the car smelled sugar sweet and Alex took a deep breath of it before putting Sara into the back, clipping in a seatbelt that looked ridiculously large on her. Closing the door shut, Alex saw that it was covered in blood, splashes like the flick of a paintbrush that long ago dribbled down and dried. Hayden was already in the driver's seat and Alex sat down beside him, slamming her door. She looked around the inside of this foreign car. It seemed clean and untouched. Hayden started driving without a word being exchanged and the breeze blew through their open windows. Within seconds the wind roared and the engine rumbled. Alex didn't dare say a thing; she knew that any gentle words would be drowned out by this noise, this wonderful noise. She didn't want to hear the echoing patter of steps, the taunts of scavenging crows, the droning buzz of a million, a billion insects. She looked over to Hayden, expecting him to pass her a glance, but he remained focused on the road ahead, his hands gripped tight to the wheel, those salty black locks flitting back behind his ears. She looked back to the kids, Caleb pale and serious, Sara hunched over and weeping. But they were there. They were in the backseat and the whole family was once again moving. She let Sara cry. She watched tears flow down each cheek before running a hand to her own face. Alex's skin was dry. She looked back to Hayden and he turned to make eye contact before swallowing and nodding. The highway was wide-open and empty. The air was clean and brisk. Fertile mountains rose up behind the fields like knees out from a bath. Trees blurred past from both sides of the road. Looking back, the wreckage was nowhere to be seen.

There was something in one of the cup holders. It was an iPhone, just like Hayden's, white-silver and gleaming—a technological triumph that felt cruel in the context of this stolen vehicle, the fermenting carnage now out of sight in behind them. Alex picked it up, her expression reflecting in the glossy black screen. The display lit up to reveal the face of a young man with a smile so gaping, so wide, that Alex could see the curled tip of his tongue. He might have been laughing. He couldn't have been more than thirty years old. She thought she might scream and threw the phone out from the open window. Hayden seemed ready to ask her something, but instead returned his focus to the highway ahead. Now she cried, thinking about that man's expression, so fucking happy, so fucking young. She knew it was stupid to cry about that one man when she'd just witnessed so much death—but all of *that* was far too incomprehensible. That was too much for any one reaction. That left her stunned, her senses washed-out and raw. Yet this man, this young, handsome man, his life was easy to grab onto and then throw away. *His life,* she could lament at this moment. And she didn't try to control the tears. Right then, Alex found contentment with crying for one dead soul. Just one.

PART
FOUR

Alex had completed this drive dozens of times before. It was nine hours of winding, climbing, descending (and repeating) through passes and valleys, dense emerald hillsides, jagged monolithic peaks, tanned hills with rows of grape vines tracing contour lines. To the left, there are rolling beige prairies with huddles of leafy trees clustered along small creeks, the bark bleached white and peeling; to the right there is a great chasm tumbling down and then back up, the distant hills those of another country. Even when stuck behind a trio of groaning semis, even with one and then a pair of unappreciative children in the backseat—even that one time Hayden forgot his CDs and they were all relegated to scouring nebulous radio reception from town to town—*even then* Alex enjoyed the journey. This highway was the antithesis of American interstates. It swerved along mountainsides with turns so sharp that speeds reduced to that of a sprint. It meandered along river valleys and through the hearts of small towns, transforming into proper (noun) Main

Streets with sparse cars parked at forty-five degree angles. Shirtless men in shorts and flip-flops would amble on the gravel shoulders with plastic bags stretched by the mass of beer cans within, a dog trundling along a few steps behind without a leash. And then for a hundred kilometers there would be no services, no billboards, nothing besides a two-lane road and mountains as far as one could see. These were lands that still felt indifferent to humanity's presence, naively unaware of just how formidable our species could be. Here, nature thought of us as a nuisance, a pest at worst, but not a plague.

That was then.

Alex stared out the window at one of those many peaks that she never knew the name of, still in the final outreaches of suburban Vancouver. After inspecting the registration information, she determined that this vehicle was owned by a woman: Sandeep Gill of Abbotsford, British Columbia. She presumed the young man on the iPhone to be Sandeep's boyfriend. They had already passed the scene of another massacre, but this time a shallow grassy median allowed access around the obstruction without them having to come to a halt. Alex told the kids to look down and she did the same, only glancing once to her right for less than a second. She saw a pile of clothes with two arms sticking out, reaching up, fingers boney and firm. That was all she could discern, one static image in a scene that blurred past at a hundred kilometers per hour. She looked back to Caleb and Sara, their eyes winced shut, faces down towards their laps. Then Hayden said that it was clear. The road ahead was empty. Clouds like stretched lace hung above jagged, frosted mountaintops. Gravel and sand beaches outlined forested islands in the Fraser River, the water rippling and tranquil. Looking at the wrinkled ridges and slopes of the mountainsides that framed the north shore of the river, Alex realized that she'd never before seen this vista with such clarity. She could discern the peaks of distant mountain ranges that hadn't seemed to exist in the past. She could discriminate the scraggily shadows of individual trees.

Caleb asked, "What happened to all those people?"

To Alex, it felt like they'd passed the last scene ten minutes ago. She cringed, wishing her son wouldn't bring this up. But she couldn't show emotion right then. Without looking back, she said, "Caleb, there are things right now that we can't be talking about. We just can't. Right now, we need to focus on driving and getting to Nan and Kevin's place as quickly as possible."

"But why—"

Alex spun around, "I said we can't. So, don't. Not now. Please." She turned to face ahead before she might break. She knew that there was no good that could come from such a discussion. If Caleb said even another word then she would snap back without pause.

They stopped at a rest area in the middle of a sprawling provincial park, sitting on the tabletops of wooden picnic benches, sipping water from one-liter bottles, tearing apart the foil wrapping on granola bars and pulling sticky clusters of red licorice into individual ropes. Sara swung her feet off the edge while Caleb watched the highway.

Hayden started throwing rocks high into the air and onto the road, watching them bounce and skitter along the asphalt before hurtling another. Caleb joined in seconds later and then so did Sara. It was a stupid game that no one in the family had ever played before. Sara giggled as a pebble somehow went behind her, hitting Hayden. Caleb was focused on the task at hand, leaning back with his right arm, bending at the knees, pointing towards the sky before catapulting the stone. Alex joined in last, watching a marbled rock vanish into thin air before resurfacing as a tumbling black hole in the blue sky, then ricocheting against the road with a hop. Another stone skittered across the blacktop before tumbling off the far shoulder. It was then that Alex noticed eyes, black and reflective like obsidian, staring at her from across the highway from within the tall, erect trunks of trees. A deer chewed on leaves from a shrub. None of the others seemed to notice, instead, throwing more stones as high as they could, scampering back when Caleb pitched one directly above. The deer looked towards the family, a cluster of green sprouting out from either side of its mouth, ears alert and forward. "Hey," Hayden said to the kids, kneeling down with an outstretched hand pointing across the highway. "Look over there." Sara asked if it was a bear and Caleb scoffed before taking tentative steps closer. Seeing her son walk across a mountain highway, Alex immediately watched for oncoming cars, ready to tell him to be careful even though they hadn't seen another driver all morning. Caleb held out his hand as if he had something to offer. Alex followed him onto the pavement, still checking both ways. Sara wanted to get closer and Hayden followed, clasping a free hand. The deer stopped chewing, inspecting the approaching horde with a dull, blank expression. It then sprung up and around, leaping into the forest with only a rustling of leaves, disappearing seconds later.

"Why did it run?" Sara asked with a sigh.

Hayden picked her up. "It was scared of us."

They looked around through the stalks of trees for

movement, for anything.

Caleb asked, "Why are there deer still but no people?"

Hayden turned to Alex, voiceless.

"Come on." Alex said, "Let's get back in. I'll drive this time."

Roadside signs indicated that the town of Princeton was ten kilometers away. Billboards advertised upcoming pubs, restaurants, and the ubiquitous small-town Subway. For the last half-hour, Hayden had successfully prodded Caleb into a game of twenty questions, luring him into the false banality of a long road-trip. Hayden's choices for objects were decidedly rural—mountain, deer, tree—while Caleb chose the Nintendo Wii, a soccer ball, a piano. Alex was nervous that Caleb's choices would bring back discussions about what happened, about home. Hayden seemed to feel the same way, countering Caleb's McDonald's with a glacier (even though Caleb didn't know what a glacier was and felt cheated that his father had chosen such an obscure object). The long descent from the Cascade Mountains was coming to an end and stout, two-story motels and gas stations were visible up ahead. Brown and withered stalks of grass stood motionless from the gravel on the sides of the highway. The late morning sun had matured and was now harsh, bleaching the town sepia. Caleb asked if they were going to stop here and neither Hayden nor Alex had an answer.

"We should at least pick up some more food," Hayden said with a volume meant to go unheard to anyone in the backseat. Alex was uneasy about stopping and hesitated to reply.

"Yeah, we should stop," Caleb said, leaning forward. "I'm so hungry."

Individual pebbles from the gravel parking lot grumbled

beneath the rolling tires. Alex said that only Hayden could go inside. Everyone else would stay with her and there would be no arguing the point. Alex told Hayden to be quick, to pick up only the essentials and to leave if there was anything wrong. He walked towards the door and gently tugged on the handle to see if it was unlocked. It was unlocked. Alex spun the car around in preparation of making a quick exit. Hayden disappeared through the glare in the gas station's windows, reappearing a few feet later around another aisle. Caleb asked what he was getting and Alex shushed. Hayden knelt to grab something and stayed down, below the lip of the window. She wanted to yell at Hayden to hurry up. She thought of hitting the horn. Looking around, the town was vacant. There was no rush. And yet she honked the horn and Hayden looked towards her from the other side of the store, nodding to ensure that he got the point. He emerged from the entrance carrying two plastic bags strained with goods. Caleb cheered and Sara clapped her hands. Hayden waited by the trunk, knocking on the metal to get Alex's attention. Open the damn thing. She scanned around for the button, impatient with every passing second that was wasted trying to figure out the details of this vehicle. Hayden returned to the passenger seat bearing gifts. A box of Smarties for Sara and a king-size Snickers for Caleb. He was the father of the year.

"Just the essentials," Hayden said, tearing off a knobby chunk from a chocolate bar, a string of caramel running to his lips. He then tossed Alex a Snickers and she opened it up before hitting the gas.

"Just the essentials," she agreed.

After Princeton, the dense forests thinned to reveal rocky

ridges and rolling blonde hills. Passing mountainsides that were once lush became almost bald, slopes sprouting withered beige grasses with sagebrush that dotted the landscape like mold on bread. Caleb and Sara slept and neither Alex nor Hayden dared to say a word. They looked out at their surroundings, appreciating this landscape that bore no signs of the atrocities of earlier.

"Look," Hayden pointed ahead with an outstretched finger, urgency in his whisper. Alex didn't know where she was being directed—his arm wavered from side to side—but then saw the starburst reflection. A windshield. A car up ahead on the highway, facing them. "It's moving. It's coming towards us."

"Shit," Alex veered towards the right shoulder. For the last hour, she'd straddled the yellow centerline. "Should we pull over?"

"Flash your headlights."

Alex tugged on a lever and activated the windshield wipers. A moment later she found the correct switch and toggled the lights. The approaching car did the same. She pulled over, hesitant to apply the brakes, but came to a complete stop as a gleaming black sports car passed and came to a halt in the middle of the opposing lane. Watching through her side-view mirror, Alex could see the movement of a single figure through the tinted windows. Hayden grabbed Alex's hand, drawing over her attention.

"Should we go?"

"Maybe we should wait and see what they do?"

Hayden craned his neck to look around, smiling at Caleb and Sara. Both cars remained still.

"What do you think they are waiting for?" Hayden asked.

"For us to do something."

"What's going on?" Caleb asked while rubbing one eye.

Hayden and Alex looked at each other, hoping that the other would give an answer. Hayden said, "We're just being careful."

Caleb watched over the back headrest, his knees dug into the corner of his seat. "Who is that?"

"We don't know," Alex said, her hand resting atop the door's lever. She pulled it open and stepped outside, peering back to Hayden to add, "Stay in here. I'll go talk." She closed the door harder than intended, silencing Hayden's reply. She walked along the pavement, the heat wafting up against her thighs. Hayden couldn't always be the brave one in front of the kids, she thought. A door opened from the other car, revealing two hairy legs clad in loose nylon shorts, white and pastel-orange sneakers that swung out and scraped against the asphalt. Two hands gripped the low opening and out stood a tall, burly man with dark skin and perfectly black hair. He smiled and waved, his teeth luminous against his complexion. There was a goofiness to his grin that allayed so many of Alex's concerns. She waved back.

"Hey." He reached out an arm to shake and Alex chuckled over the formality. "My name's Simar."

"I'm Alex." She turned back, "And that's my husband, Hayden, and two kids, Caleb and Sara."

"Cool." He waved towards Hayden, his expression almost meek. "Where you guys coming from?"

"Vancouver."

"Shit. Vancouver? All you guys came from Vancouver?" He was clearly surprised.

"Yeah," Alex nodded, unsure why this was worthy of such exclaim.

"You're the first people I've met from a city. That's crazy."

"Why is that crazy?"

"Because," Simar shrugged, expelling a nervous chuckle. "Because the only people I've met were from, like, not even villages. Just random houses on backcountry roads."

"So, you've met others?"

"A few."

"Where are you from?"

"Oh, I'm from San Jose, but I was driving up to Oregon when it happened."

Footsteps scratched against the pavement from behind Alex. Hayden approached and waved.

Alex didn't wait for Hayden before asking Simar: "You know what happened?"

"Shit. No, no, no. I mean, I got my ideas, but that's all. I just assumed that no one got out of the cities," Simar wasn't finished his sentence; his lips and tongue lingered but didn't make a sound, reluctant to complete his thought. "You must be Hayden? I'm Simar."

"Nice car you got there, Simar. What is that? A Cayenne?"

He looked back towards the vehicle and laughed. "Yeah, I think that's what it's called. I hate to say, it's not really my car. I've had to," Simar paused to think of the word, "borrow different vehicles over these last few days. You know, it's less messy than syphoning gas."

"I know exactly what you're talking about," Hayden answered.

Simar smiled, inspecting the white Volkswagon Golf, the splatters of blood still visible on the doors. "Yeah? Then I guess I've got much better taste than you guys."

*   *   *

The sun was punishing, casting dark, tight shadows that framed the base of shrubs and outlined each of the scraggily cracks that snaked along exposed boulders. Caleb helped Sara climb an embankment, her feet slipping against the loose gravel and shale, up towards a barren ridge and sparse barbwire fence that bowed from one lanky wooden post to the next. The kids were given explicit instructions not to cross and neither dared to go beyond, both equally as nervous as their parents about wandering too far off. Caleb threw a stone up the hill and watched it roll back, skittering against exposed rock and disappearing into a cluster of stout, olive-leaved bushes.

The raised hatchback of the Golf acted as a parasol for Alex as she sat against the lip of the back bumper. Simar and Hayden seemed unaffected by the sunlight, each standing on the highway, taking swigs from plastic bottles of water that Simar had retrieved from a stack in the back of his Porsche. He admitted that it was hardly the most sensible vehicle, but he also figured that it would be fun to drive. So, fuck it. "Went more than a hundred and fifty miles per hour at one point," he said, shaking his head from side to side as if hypnotized. "I scared myself shitless doing that."

Although taller than anyone else, Simar's slouched posture implied that he didn't know how to wield the expansiveness of his own body. His chuckle was nervous, always short and abbreviated, while his eyes batted down towards his bright sneakers and then a random spot in the landscape. When he said that he was a software engineer, Alex wasn't at all surprised, having worked with dozens of people just like him back when she coordinated digital-effects projects. She was glad that the first person they met that day was someone harmless, someone who could admit to feeling terrified behind the wheel of a speeding sports car, someone who apologized after swearing in front of the kids, someone awkward with small-talk and nervous to bring up the most important questions. He prodded a stone between his shoes while asking how they managed to get out of a city, confessing that he was just lucky; he was already far away from anywhere when he started hearing about the events of August 14th. "The radio kept calling these *terrorist attacks*," he said, "but that didn't seem right. The same thing was happening in big cities and small towns all over the world. I knew it wasn't terrorists. That was just a knee-jerk reaction. I didn't know what it was, but it seemed obvious that this wasn't Al Qaeda or something. I mean, why the hell would terrorists take on Deer Lake, Texas? Or that village in Indonesia? Or China? Or Peru? I mean, what terrorist group out there has a problem with Peru?" He chuckled and then looked back down, "Sorry, I shouldn't be laughing about any of this."

"What happened in Peru?" Alex asked. "Or Indonesia?"

"There's been lots of these little things going on, little test runs and shit for the last few weeks. Long before Texas. A lot of it didn't make the major news but you could find things online. I spend a lot of time—I used to spend a lot of time—reading stuff online. In Peru, an entire village jumped off a cliff. Not a single person left alive. And there was a town in Indonesia where everyone killed each other, but not with guns or machetes and shit, but with their bare hands. I saw photos of this stuff posted online. And I figured that for every town we heard about, it must have happened in several other places, you know? I mean, there must have been hundreds of these things all over the world. But that's what us Americans do. We just blame everything on terrorists. It's always fucking Osama, right? But this ain't terrorists." He shook his head, eyes down on his shoes. He then repeated, perhaps for emphasis, perhaps just to fill the silence. "This ain't terrorists."

"So, what is it?" Alex asked.

Simar laughed, shaking his head. "How many times have we asked that, right? I have my guesses, but you know what? The only question that really matters is: what do we need to do to stay alive? That's all that matters. And if you ask me, I think we need to stay right fucking clear of cities. I tell you, I've met like," Simar paused, "ten people since this started, and you're the only ones from a city. I haven't even met anyone from a town. Until you guys, the only survivors were those living way off the beaten track. Every time I drive through a town, it reeks of death. Literally. Just a stench. Even the smallest of places. So, what does that tell us? It's not safe to be close to any center of population. That's why I'm steering clear of Interstates and major highways. That's why I'm here, in Canada, and driving north. And that's what I recommend for you guys—go north, get as far away from towns or other people as you can."

Sara started crying and all the adults looked up toward the hill to find her on her hands and knees. Hayden jogged up the incline and picked her up, brushing off the dirt. Alex said to Simar: "He didn't believe me in the days before. I knew something was up. I could feel it." She held up her left finger, the scab dry and flaky. "About a week before it happened, I cut myself, but I wasn't thinking about anything. I didn't even notice. It was like my thoughts were—"

"—interrupted?"

Alex expelled a snorting, beleaguered laugh.

Simar nodded. "Yeah, I know exactly what you mean. I've felt it while driving. On The Fourteenth and days since. People

I've met said that same thing. I even read about it online too, before it happened. People in Deer Lake, near the office building, said that they felt drugged. Like they were sleepwalking. But when they went to the hospital, there was nothing in their bloodstream."

"The day it happened, I knew something was wrong and I got us all out of there. I knew something was wrong, I just didn't know what." Alex shook her head. "I still don't know what."

Up on the embankment, Hayden held Sara up in his arms, directing her towards some point across the valley as he spoke into her ear, his words unheard to anyone else. Simar said, "I think it's some sort of mind-control. Why else would people jump off a cliff? Into a lake? Drive their cars off the side of the road? Attack each other? I think us—you, me, your family— we've been on the edge of something, like outer ring of a blast radius, you know? Close enough to feel it, but not so close to lose complete control." He sniffled and Alex noticed the glaze over his eyes. He tried to look away and she didn't want to draw attention to it, glancing back towards Hayden and the kids. He continued, "I'm sure you've seen some awful shit. I would have never thought that I could have gone through with the things that I've done in just the last few days, you know? I had to," Simar stopped, wincing, shaking his head. "The smell—it was like kimchi. That's what I thought. Fucking kimchi. But you do it. You know you don't have a choice, so you fucking do it. You can't think about those things. You have to just keep driving. That's why I just want to keep going north. I don't want to see that shit anymore."

Alex was brought back to that very morning, sprinting along the highway alongside the wreckage of thousands of vehicles and lives. The one image she couldn't shake was the young girl with cavernous gaps where there were once eyes. "When do you think you'll stop?"

"I don't know. I want to find a cabin on a plot of land. By a stream with fresh water. Grow some vegetables. Live like that. Maybe find someone else who knows what the fuck they're doing—I can't even cook, let alone grow stuff."

"What about friends? Family? What about going back?"

Simar wiped his eyes and looked down to Alex. He started with a couple of different replies, "You think," followed by, "What do you—" He shook his head and tried again. "I don't think there can be a going back. I don't think that I have friends or family left." His words staggered by the end and Alex apologized. "No, no, don't say you're sorry. This isn't just me. This is everyone. I sincerely hope that you find your mother— and if she lives in a small place off a lake, away from a town, then she's probably fine—but I'm sure as hell not going to find mine again. That's just the way it is. Not going to do any good getting emotional."

Simar was holding back tears and Alex wanted to tell him to stop being so selfish, to go back and try and find his family. She couldn't understand how this young man could flee from everyone he knew with such ease. Such callousness. For someone who counted himself as being lucky for being alive, why would he relegate himself to an existence of solitude so quickly? It was a cop out. The reaction of a scared and sheltered (six-foot-five) boy. Simar apologized again for "getting emotional" and Alex told him that it was natural, that it was nothing to be ashamed of. And when she said this, she felt no urge to cry herself. Not at that time, for right then she felt sorry for Simar. He had nothing but a stolen sports car and a plan to drive as far north as possible. She, at least, still had hope. She had family.

"You know," Alex said, "at any time, you could turn around and drive back. Try to find your family. You're free to do whatever you want."

Simar looked down to Alex, his eyes teary and now disappointed. "I'm sure you've seen what I've seen. I don't want to see that again. I like this, out here in the middle of nowhere. Standing here, right here, this feels normal. I like this. The reason we are alive is because we didn't try to do something stupid like driving back to a city. That's why we are alive. I'm certain of that."

"How can you be certain of anything? You said yourself you don't know what's going on."

"Well, I'm certain of that much. It's one of the few things left, but I'm certain of it."

"How?"

"Because I'm still alive. I've been driving for three days, in and out of small roads, getting lost, and I've met ten people. Ten. That includes you four. And all of them have kept far away from anyone else. That's my proof."

"That's not proof," Alex said, surprised how those few words quivered, revealing her fragility. She felt such fortitude mere moments earlier, but now she thought of her mother, what she would do if she made it to Kootenay Lake only to find her... Alex wouldn't allow herself to finish that thought. She had held it back for days now. There was no way of knowing until she drove more. Another five hours, if all went well.

Simar apologized again and this time Alex didn't remind him not to. He should be sorry for saying such things, she thought. He then chuckled a forced, deprecating laugh. Before

Alex could ask, he pointed to an ant scampering along the pavement between his shoes. "So, just a couple of weeks ago, I woke up and my kitchen was infested in ants. Little black ones. There were like thousands of them. So, I went to the store and bought this ant killer. Put drops all around where they frequented. The instructions said that the ants take some of the poison and return it to the nest where it kills the entire colony. I watched as those pathetic little insects swarmed the drops, nudging one another to the sides just to get a little bit more. I'd make a point of coming back just to check up, kneeling down to watch them eat the poison before scampering back off towards their nest. I even tried following them back, just to see where the colony was. It felt good to watch them. They had no idea that I was right there, towering over, beholding hundreds of them all at the same time. I'd mutter at them, as if I was taunting. *Take that, you fuckers.* It was the first thing I checked the next morning, to see if those ants were still there. And there were only a few stragglers, like two or three per drop. And the day after that: all gone. Not a single one. And I felt great about it." Simar forced out another chuckle. "Take that, you fuckers." The lone ant on the asphalt crawled over the lip of the road and into the gravel.

"You think we're the ants?"

Simar nodded.

"Then who are they?"

He shrugged, almost dismissive. "Do you think it mattered who I was to the ants in my apartment? That my name is Simar Virk? That I'm a human being?"

"But we're not ants, Simar."

"Maybe to them, we are." Simar waited to see if Alex would reply. "Don't pretend that you haven't thought about it.

I know you have. I can see it on your face. What else could it be?"

Alex stared at Hayden up the hill with Sara on his shoulders. She could hear her giggle, pretending to beg for her Daddy to stop. "We're not ants."

"You're right. We're smarter than ants. And if I was an ant who knew that some human wanted me dead, the first thing I would do is get the hell out of his house. And I would probably get the hell out of his yard. And I would go as far away as I could from all the other ants, because as soon as a colony gets too big, I know one of those crazy ass humans is going to have no problems, whatsoever, with killing us all."

Simar had warned Alex about the town of Osoyoos, a conglomeration of Mediterranean-themed motels split into two halves on either side of a lake in the country's lone desert valley. There was only one way through: a ruler-straight road that cut across the azure water upon an extension of a sandbar. Although the highway was unobstructed, Simar said that the surrounding lake must have had more than a thousand bodies floating in it. But the road was clear, he repeated several times. Just drive fast, and you should be fine. Tell the kids not to look.

On the outskirts of the town, they passed an empty gas station with cars still waiting at the pumps. Without asking, Hayden spun around and pulled over into the parking lot, whispering to Alex how he wasn't sure if they'd have enough gas to make it to the next town. Hayden went from vehicle to vehicle, each with unlocked doors, many left wide open. A charcoal Jeep still had the gasoline nozzle inserted into the tank, the black hose hanging like an umbilical cord to the pump. Minutes later, they'd taken possession of a minivan with a full twenty-gallon tank. The keys were in the ignition and when Hayden twisted it on, Raffi's "Baby Beluga" played over the speakers. An empty child seat with twisted straps and crumbled Cheerios occupied a leather chair with foldable armrests beside the sliding side door. Alex pulled out the hooks and threw it on the pavement. The back row was packed with luggage. "Let's just get going," Hayden said, not wanting to discard everything or spend time sorting through this family's belongings. Caleb found a Nintendo DS under his seat and asked to play it. Hayden gave him the okay before Alex could reply. "We have much bigger things to worry about," Hayden said as if to remind her. Alex knew, of course, and yet it still seemed so wrong. That was a dead child's toy. Her foot crumpled on the wrapper for a package of infant rice biscuits, the type of crackers that dissolve upon contact with saliva. It was the same brand that Sara used to demand.

"Just drive fast," she told Hayden.

Crossing the lake, Alex instructed the kids to look at the ground while she sat sideways on her seat, staring back and watching the space between her children's feet. But Caleb didn't listen, continually glancing out towards the lake and the motionless figures that floated in the water like driftwood. "Caleb!" Alex yelled, but he wouldn't relent. "Caleb, fucking listen to me." She wanted to hit him. He'd never before been so disobedient. He didn't even blink. His eyes locked on something in the middle. No one thing seemed to stand out, the wrinkled surface of the water broken with corpses that bore little detail under the glaring afternoon sun. Another stucco-clad beige motel blocked his view and Caleb turned his head to stare straight ahead, his eyes not once connecting with Alex's.

"Caleb," Alex began, her tone now defeated. She didn't

know what else to say. "You shouldn't see that."

"It doesn't matter if I see it or not," he then said. "It doesn't stop it from being there."

Alex waited for him to look at her. He didn't. He stared out his window towards the bleached roads and parallel curves of vineyards that traced the nooks and crooks of hillsides. The engine whined as Hayden took the minivan up a set of switchbacks that clung to the side of a precipitous valley, each 180-degree turn offering a panoramic view of the entire lake. From up here, the water seemed nearly unspoiled; a matte finish that reflected only the washed-out colors from the steep, barren mountainsides. And then, after one last turn, the lake was gone. Alex looked back, hoping Caleb might offer some apology, either in words or with his expression. He flipped open the DS and resumed playing.

Manila hills turned green, puffs of sagebrush replaced with arrowhead evergreen trees, first in coniferous clumps and then a ceaseless, unbroken forest. Ostensibly random and irregular polygons cut conspicuous holes in the mountainsides, the exposed forest floors remnants of clear-cut logging operations. Towns passed by every half-hour, assemblies of a few inactive traffic lights, a sparse grid of roads, a gas station. Maybe two. At times, humble pre-war wooden houses faced the highway, the front steps seemingly just out of reach from the minivan, their front yards a spectrum of green grass to pebble gravel. Hayden would honk the horn, looking back in the rearview mirror to see if any screen doors would open. Any people might emerge, waving their arms. No one did. To Alex, these small, forgettable towns delineated the passage of time. When they skimmed the east shore of Christina Lake, its ruffled water imitating a meandering fjord, she knew that there were less than three hours left. A single white boat caught Hayden and Alex's attention and they struggled to see if there was anyone on board, but it was too distant. The rest of the lake appeared unblemished. Usually, this view from the highway would taunt her, urging her to pull over and jump into the water. But right then, she wanted to move on. As clean and immaculate as the lake appeared, it was surely tainted. She felt grateful for the stands of trees that blocked her view of any potential details. They began the next ascent to Bonanza Pass. Less than three hours.

The kids were sleeping. When Hayden said, "What if Barbara is not there?" it seemed to break Alex out from a dream; it had been so long since anyone said a word.

Alex was in no rush to reply and Hayden didn't expect an immediate answer. His eyes remained focused on the road ahead. "What do you mean?" she asked, almost recoiling from her choice of words.

Hayden shook his head slowly. "What if we get there and the place is empty?"

Alex thought that he would ask something else. *What if she is dead?* "I guess we'll see when we get there."

"We're just a few hours away now."

"I know how far we are."

"Then I think we should talk about it before. We should have a plan."

"Why can't we just talk about it when we get there? Right now, we don't know anything. She could be fine."

"Of course." Hayden's words sounded conclusive. He had let the topic go. Alex closed her eyes, listening to the muffled rumble of the engine and her children's gentle breaths in behind.

She couldn't fault him for asking. She had been asking herself the very same question for the last few days, always casting it aside with the condition that such thoughts were moot until they knew more. And he couldn't appreciate what it meant for her to see her mother again; Hayden wasn't close with either of his parents. She doubted they even knew that Hayden had fathered a second child. For him, the west coast was an escape, a fresh-start from his old life. For Alex, this was her home.

He then said, "But I still think we should have some idea about what to do, just in case."

Alex groaned. Her goodwill was evaporating. "Why? Why can't we wait three hours?"

"Because," Hayden clearly knew what he wanted to say, but hesitated after that first word, glancing over to check Alex's expression. "Because we've seen some awful things."

"I know."

"And we need to be prepared for the worst."

As if Hayden had thrust a picture in front of her face, a horrible visual surfaced in her imagination. She didn't want it there, she didn't wish to think about this, but he wouldn't relent. Alex's mother was face down in the lake, feet from the gravel shore. She was dressed in that mauve fleece jacket—the one she wore for half the damn year, every year, for the last ten years— sopping wet and twinkling under the summer sun. The water around her didn't ripple, didn't have a single wave or crinkle. Her feet were bare and wrinkled. The lake was so calm that she didn't bob. Something flicked the water in the distance; a jostling fish sprung a series of circular ripples along the surface. And still her mother didn't move. Alex's eyes were open and she couldn't shake this image. She felt tears swell and this made her angry with Hayden. This was his fault. Why did he want her to cry again? What purpose was this serving? "What do you want me to say?"

"I don't want you to say anything. I just want to be prepared."

"What does that mean?"

Hayden grimaced, eyes fixed on the road ahead. He answered, "This whole time, from the very beginning, you've said that we're going out to find Barbara. It was never up for discussion, it was never up for debate and I went along with it. As a family, we all went along with it from the very beginning as if there was no other choice. As if it was the best choice. But we have to be honest with each other. There's a very good chance that she won't be there. Or worse. And we have never—never once—discussed what might happen then."

"Why can't we just wait?"

"Because it's going to be so much harder to think about things then."

"You think she's gone?"

"I do."

Alex didn't expect his decisiveness. His answer was without hesitation. She almost laughed from bewilderment. "You seem pretty certain about that."

"I think what Simar said was right."

"That we're fucking ants?"

"That we need to go north."

"Do you think that it's a mistake, us going to Kootenay Lake?"

"I'm afraid that it might turn into a mistake."

"And what does that mean?"

Hayden glanced back to Caleb and Sara, checking to see if they were still asleep. "We've witnessed enough as it is. I don't want you to see what might have happened to your mother. No one should see that, not you, not the kids."

"So, you think we should have followed Simar?"

Hayden didn't reply.

"You think we're just ants," Alex said, prodding him.

After a protracted pause, Hayden answered. "It wouldn't be the craziest thought I've had these last few days."

They descended into the Creston valley at the nape of Kootenay Lake. In between mountainsides, this land was as uniform as open prairie, vast agricultural fields sown from the deposits of the glacier fed lake upstream. The unforgiving late afternoon sun cast down onto this linear stretch of highway, conjuring imaginary puddles on the dry, barren pavement. Alex lowered her window and held out her fingers, the air blasting through her fingertips like a hair dryer. When Caleb asked if they were almost there, Alex laughed. It felt cliché; a family on a road trip traversing the province in a minivan, a bored child asking the most predictable of questions. "It's not much longer now," she said, relishing in this moment of banality, of routine, of the ordinary. And it was this familiarity that gave Alex some measure of hope. Less than an hour away was her mother's cabin. Barbara and Kevin could very well be waiting for her. There were no more towns to traverse—soon they would take their last left and meander up the east shore of Kootenay Lake.

A vehicle emerged from the lip of a hill in the highway ahead, tires straddling either side of the yellow line. Alex thought that it could Barbara. It could be Kevin. Her mind raced with what she knew were ridiculous and outlandish thoughts. She sat forwards, her hands on the dash. She heard long blasts of the approaching horn—five, six, seven times in a row. It was a 90's era SUV with a rusted and bleached red paint job, the sun reflecting against its tinted windows, obscuring those within. The front license plate was missing. Hayden had already parked in the shoulder but the SUV approached as if ready to pass before spinning forty-five degrees, obstructing both lanes ahead, and stopped with a jittering squeal.

"What the fuck," Hayden said.

Alex looked back to the kids, hoping they might somehow not be seeing this. Caleb asked what was going on and Alex only shook her head. She then tried to whisper to Hayden in a way that Caleb wouldn't hear. "I don't like this."

"I know." Hayden's foot remained an inch above the gas.

"They're trying to block us, aren't they?"

Hayden didn't respond, attempting to peer through the glare.

Alex said, "Maybe you should just drive?"

"Their engine is still running. They can stop us too easily."

The passenger door of the opposing SUV opened but no one exited. "Stay in the car," Alex said.

"I'm not going anywhere."

The door hung open, as if an invitation for someone to enter. Alex could make out movement through the windshield.

"I think you should hit the gas and drive right past them," she said.

"We're in a minivan. We can't escape."

The SUV's back door then opened and pairs of shoes pressed against the cracked pavement. Seconds later, two men stepped out in unison, both dressed in t-shirts and shorts, one with tattoos muddying both arms, one with a black ball cap aligned firmly forward. Each had a strap slung over one shoulder. There was that naïve, ephemeral moment where Alex expected them to carry backpacks. It was in that moment—in what was surely less than a single second—when she inspected their faces, judged the men to be in their twenties, noted the density of the man's tattoos and the defined muscles of the other's calves. Jogger's legs. And then they pulled around the rifles that had hung in behind, gripping their weapons with both hands. Her stomach shriveled before she made a sound, before she gasped. A pang of nausea fired up her throat. They had guns. Her children were in the back. The men walked with a strut, flaunting their firearms. The one with the tattoos scowled, as if acting. The athlete led the way, a couple paces ahead. Dark hair sprouted out from the sides of his Oakland Raider's cap, curling around the seam and behind his ears. He then smiled, revealing a pair of wide, square front teeth. His rifle wasn't pointed at anything, but still he held it with both hands, his eyes making unwavering contact with Hayden's. Steps from the minivan, he rolled an imaginary lever with one hand. Caleb asked if those were guns. Alex didn't want to answer but Caleb repeated himself. "We're going to be okay," she said, wishing she could think of something better, something that wasn't so clearly insincere.

Hayden lowered the window.

"Hey," said the man with the Raider's cap, still smiling, deep dimples in each cheek, accenting his brief greeting with a nod. He let his rifle droop downwards towards the asphalt. He then looked towards Alex and smiled a little wider, his eyes wincing, a pose for a camera. "Where you guys going?" he asked Hayden, casual. They were two men waiting in an airport lounge.

"We're," Hayden began, his voice hoarse. He cleared his throat to try again, but remained lost for words.

126

The man laughed, "Don't let the guns scare you," he paused as if there was nothing else to say about that and glanced towards Alex. "We like to be careful. We've seen some crazy shit and don't really know what to expect. You know what I mean?"

"Yes," Hayden cleared his throat again, "Of course."

The other man sauntered around the minivan, his shoes scraping long steps along the pavement, eyes searching every window from every angle.

Caleb asked if these men were from the army and the man chuckled, peering his head in to see the backseat. "We're not quite military, young man." His eyes then swung side to side to make contact with both Hayden and Alex. "So, where you all heading? You're the first people we've seen today."

Hayden glanced towards Alex, "We're going to her mother's, hoping that they're okay."

"Where she live?"

"Moyie Lake," Hayden answered. "We've been driving for hours, just hoping she's okay."

Alex's heart shuddered, unsure why Hayden lied, scared that Caleb might say something about this.

"Where abouts? Which part of town?"

Hayden shook his head, "Shit, I can't remember the exact name of the road. I think it's Braid? Look, do you guys know what's been going on?"

He chuckled and shook his head. "My boy here heard something about terrorists, but that's all. Not that it matters, right?" The man leaned in again, looked at the dash and then towards Alex. "You're awfully quiet there, lady. Nothing to say?"

Alex shook her head.

"Well, I don't think you're going to have enough gas to make it to Moyie Lake."

"Look," Hayden leaned towards the man, directing his words out the window and lowering his voice to a whisper. "My kids are scared. They're really scared. I don't know what we're going to do about gas, but we're going to have to figure it out. I just don't want to scare them anymore, you know?"

The man nodded, running his tongue over his teeth, eyes continually returning to Alex. Never before had she felt so powerless, so feeble. She didn't have the mettle to say a word to the man. She couldn't maintain eye contact. She looked down at her lap, her feet, feeling her heart wallop her ribs with the thump of a kick drum, her stomach tight. Sara started asking what was going on, her tone both whining and pleading. Alex looked back and couldn't think of a word to say to her daughter that wasn't a complete and terrible lie. She could only shush. When she caught the expression of Caleb—eyes strained and focused on the man standing outside Hayden's door—Alex thought of how they might die right here. There was nothing stopping these people from shooting Hayden. In front of her children. It didn't matter what they'd then do to her, it was the idea that Caleb and Sara might witness their parents come to an end in plain sight, strapped into their seats. Alex didn't want to cry but the tears burst out while looking at Caleb. After all they'd been through, this wasn't fucking fair. Sara started to moan and Alex wanted to be in the backseat with them. The kids shouldn't have been left on their own.

"I'm sorry," Alex then said towards the man with the Raider's cap, the leader, her words sounding anything but apologetic. "If there's nothing more to say, we really need to get going. Please, I need to see my mother. We need to get going."

The man nodded, his right cheek curling into a conciliatory smile.

"Please," Alex repeated.

He looked towards his partner and their idling SUV. He tapped the roof of the car twice. "Well, you guys should get going to Moyie Lake then, right?"

"Thank you," Hayden said over Sara's sobs.

Alex didn't offer any acknowledgments, impatient for Hayden to start driving.

"You guys just be careful out there," the man said and Hayden thanked him again before accelerating cautiously, veering around their vehicle, the right wheels of the minivan grumbling over gravel in the shoulder. As soon as they were clear, Hayden picked up speed but wouldn't floor the gas. The minivan's transmission progressed up the gears. Alex watched through the rearview mirror, the two figures on the road strolling back towards their truck, no one in a rush.

"What the fuck was that?" Alex expelled, her words breathy, her eyes transfixed on the reflection in the mirror, afraid that the SUV was going to turn and follow.

Hayden shook his head, still accelerating. Up ahead, the highway appeared to conclude at a stand of trees that delineated the base of a mountain. Alex could no longer see far enough back to tell if those men had gone on their way, were still blocking the middle of the highway, or had decided to give chase. A sign directed traffic to turn right for the town of Creston. Moyie Lake was another hour past that. Hayden applied the brakes just enough to take a ninety-degree turn left without hurtling off the road. Caleb was shushing Sara and Alex sat to the side, her neck craned towards the road behind. Once around, Hayden bore no caution, hitting the gas hard enough to propel people into their seats. Caleb again asked who those men were and Alex shook her head. "I don't know."

"Were they bad?"

"They weren't good."

"Why did they have guns?"

"Not now, Caleb. Not now." Alex sat forward, the highway swerving to follow the twisting shoreline and adjacent mountainside. Each turn obscured any sign of someone following, granting both a sense of privacy but also one of uncertainty; each meandering curve could straighten out to reveal those men in their rusted SUV, approaching from behind.

Alex asked Hayden, "Why did you say we were going to Moyie?"

"I didn't think they needed to know the truth."

"Is there a Braid street there?"

Hayden shrugged his shoulders. "Doubt it."

"What do you think those two are doing?"

"Three." Hayden corrected. "At least three. There was a driver that we never saw. Who knows who else was in the back."

"Why do you think they were walking around with guns?"

"Because they can? I don't know. I just want to get the fuck away from there."

Sara's cries had reduced to whimpers, her feet now dangling, her chin down to her chest. Alex slipped between the seats, picked up her daughter and laid her down on her lap.

"Mom," Caleb asked, seeking approval before saying anything more. "Were they going to hurt us?"

"We're safe now, Caleb."

"Are we almost there yet?"

"We're almost there, Caleb. We're almost there." And for

once, Alex didn't feel like she was lying to her son. And for once, she wanted Barbara's cabin to be farther away, beyond yet another mountain range, past one last nestled valley. Somewhere far removed and secluded from those men with their conspicuous guns. But after nine hours of driving, after two days in an isolated house overlooking Mount Baker, after the trauma, after the terror, after everything they had been through, the Maclean family was only fifteen minutes away from their destination.

Kootenay Lake sparkled, its water reflecting the undeveloped mountainside across to the other shore. To Alex, this was the most pristine, the most enchanted place in the entire world. She always let Hayden take this part of the drive so that she could admire the vistas between stands of trees. Now, she was nervous to admire the water too long, afraid of what she might discover. She kept her focus towards the middle of the lake, to those sheets of smooth, gently warped cellophane. She struggled to recall the day of the week. It was Thursday. They left on a Tuesday. Hayden didn't ask any questions, reaching across to hold her knee and then hands. But she didn't need any consoling. They knew nothing. They passed a handmade sign advertising lake-view lots for sale, the word "WOW!" painted in a red starburst. Barbara and Kevin lived at the very next left-hand turn, down a gravel road that slunk between cedars, switching back once and then twice. The steepness of the driveway forced people into their seatbelts. The blue glimmer of the lake was barely visible through a dense swath of trees. There was no sign of Barbara's sedan but Kevin's truck, its paint a faded black as if coated in dust, remained parked by the back, adjacent to a pile of firewood draped in a pine-needle covered tarp. The front door of the house was closed. Hayden motioned towards the truck, said that someone might be home, and Alex nodded, her throat too dry to reply. Hayden pulled up and turned off the ignition, letting Alex make the first move.

She needed just one more moment. She was hoping that someone would have come to greet them. She stepped out and Hayden did the same, telling the kids to wait. Alex walked to the front door and it was locked. She knocked on windows while pulling up the cover for the barbecue on the deck, knowing that the spare key was hidden beneath the propane tank. She opened the door and called out with an expectant but desperate, "Mom, Kevin?" How she wanted to hear a rustle, an answer. There was no reply. Alex called out again. She took every corner with care, sniffing the air, remembering the vinegar pinch of rot from the highway. Instead she smelled nothing but that subtle must that always accompanied this space, the odor of clothes that dry over the back of a chair, draped atop an open door. The kitchen and living room opened up to the loft above, the exposed beams of the roof echoing her words back down upon her. There was too little space for anyone to go unheard and Alex stopped speaking. It was clear that no one was home. No one living, at least. The door to the downstairs bedroom was open and the bed was made, the sheets tight, awaiting guests. Caleb and Sara had wandered in, asking where Nan and Kevin were, but no one answered their questions. Alex climbed the steps, telling the kids to wait with Hayden. A single flight opened to the loft, a pair of empty armchairs faced the triangle points of the lakefront window. The master bedroom door was closed. Alex gently knocked with the tips of her knuckles, not sure why she would do such a thing. She turned the knob and inched the door forward. The sheets laid unfolded across the bed, a duvet dangling down to the carpet. Each pillow still had the divot from a night's rest. But her mother and stepfather were not home.

PART
FIVE

Snug within the crook between her mother's thighs, Sara flipped the page and insisted that she be the one who read the book. Alex acquiesced and Sara pointed to the first word at the top of the page before asking what it was. Alex said, "The next little car—" and Sara slapped the paper, reminding her that it was *her* turn. Alex apologized with a snorting chuckle, kissed Sara along the part in her hair, rested her chin on the girl's shoulder. Right then, no demand of Sara could be unjustified or inexcusable. The girl's experiences had earned her these moments of irrationality and Alex smiled, content to have her right there, so close and secure. "Okay then, go ahead."

Her daughter's feet were inches from the window, through which Alex admired the calm and glimmering sheen of Kootenay Lake between rusty trunks of cedars. Ever since Barbara moved here with Kevin, this was Alex's favorite spot, up in the loft where others were reluctant to traverse. Her mother and Kevin spent their waking hours in the living room and dining room, eyes to the television or backs to the window, never sitting in these reclining chairs that overlooked the very lake that they chose to reside along. Alex remembered sitting with Sara in this exact spot, not even a year earlier. It was late September, when the clouds first became stubborn and slothful, lumbering in uninvited and then staying for days. No one else was at the cabin—Barbara and Kevin were out while Hayden remained home with Caleb—and Alex was staring out the window when Sara started singing a muddled, toddler rendition of "The Itsy-Bitsy Spider," her two hands waving back and forth in an attempt to recreate the actions with her stubby, ungainly fingers. Alex sang along, her thumbs and index fingers tracing the imaginary spider's journey upwards. Then Alex saw what had inspired her daughter: a motionless and improbably huge arachnid splayed out on the window, each of its eight legs so large that she could make out the knuckles in its joints. She fought back an urge to shriek, amazed with the fortitude wrought from having a child sit on her lap. "Oh, look at that," Alex said as if it was something cute. A chipmunk manically biting through the shell of a nut. She lifted up Sara and placed her on the armchair while standing, asking her to stay put. "The spider won't hurt you, but just don't touch it. Mommy's going to put it somewhere safe." Even if Sara was not a witness, this creature seemed too substantial to crush under a paper towel. She hurried downstairs to retrieve a glass and plate from the kitchen. Returning to the loft, she secured the rim around the spider, its legs unflinching until she slid the cup down and prodded it into the base. Once in, Alex sealed it shut with the plate. Sara wanted a closer look and Alex brought the glass down towards her, but as soon as the spider scurried around the circumference of its prison, Sara shook her head and made it clear that she no longer wanted the being to be anywhere near her. Alex carried it out onto the deck and then over the railing. Turning over the glass, the creature tumbled towards the ferns and soil. For a moment, Alex couldn't see where it landed and she jolted back, afraid that it might have fallen between her bare feet. But her eyes caught two, four, and then all eight of its limbs reaching over the lip of the wooden planter box before vanishing over the edge. Sara asked if it was home now, and Alex said, "Yes, it's home now," with a soothing assurance. "It's back with his family."

Sara threw the book down onto the floor and said that she was too hungry to continue reading. Alex assured her daughter that she would find something to eat. Descending the steps that overlooked the fireplace and dormant television, Alex's eyes caught sight of Hayden and Caleb out along the lakeshore, twenty paces out from the front deck. Hayden whipped his right arm as he skipped an unseen stone. Caleb did the same, crouching down to watch the trail of strikes unfurl along the calm lake water, a necklace of expanding, wavering pearls. Alex walked towards the kitchen, the main counter and adjacent dining room table covered with bags of snacks and stuffed animals that once belonged to another family. The Zhang family, according to the insurance in the minivan's glovebox. Alex gripped her hand around the fridge's handle and pulled it open. The light came on and a burst of cool air tumbled out onto her arms and down to her bare feet. Even though it had been more than an hour since Hayden started the generator, this still felt novel to Alex: an appliance that worked. Caleb cheered when the power first came on—a series of pendant lights above the kitchen island flickered on without a sound—then Alex and Sara followed along, clapping their hands and hollering in approval as Hayden stepped inside. The Maclean family hero.

The first thing he did was turn on the television, revealing nothing but hissing static and blank screens. Caleb ran upstairs and powered up the computer while the rest of the family stood around, Sara peering over the lip of the desk as a flashing white cursor gave way to the Windows logo, three azure blocks swiping across a progress bar. For those seconds, Alex felt hopeful; with power came progress. The screen filled with a portrait of the Maclean family from last Christmas, taken just down the stairs in front of a crackling fire. Barbara was seated at the front with Sara between her arms. It was a terrible photo—not only was the lighting muted, but Alex glanced off to her right and Hayden's expression was blurred. And yet this was chosen to remain the desktop photograph for more than nine months. Hayden instructed Caleb to check the Internet but no connection could be established. Before Caleb was able to successfully load a game, Hayden told him that they had to conserve energy. When the propane ran out, so would their electricity.

It seemed obvious that Barbara and Kevin had purposely left, having taken her sedan and locking the doors. They had made a point of driving somewhere, but there were few clues as to when they had departed. There was nothing left in the fridge to rot—no milk or meat—and so Alex assumed that they must have been around for at least a day or two after August 14th. Stacks of portioned meat in the deep freeze were still cool to the touch, but not frozen. When Alex mentioned that they should stay here for at least a few days, Hayden seemed to agree with a pair of conciliatory nods. They had food and they had power. Alex could forgive herself at times for feeling comfortable.

That evening, a fog of smoke billowed up and highlighted the angled rays of sunlight between the trees. The searing crackle of chicken skin and hissing of dripping fat was a welcoming sound to Alex as her entire family stood around the charcoal barbecue; a feast was in order, Hayden had deemed, and no one voiced opinions to the contrary. With a glass of wine in hand, Alex gazed through the barcode of shadows that quivered, feeling as if she was underwater, the hazy forest just above the surface from where she floated. She walked up the gravel driveway towards the narrow highway, her eyes watching smoke delineate the shadows of every one of those hundreds, those thousands of trees. She stared towards the mountaintops across the lake, the sky a perfect indigo, not a cloud to be found. There was nothing to see and yet she kept watching, then walking, her sandals scraping on the asphalt. Alex no longer thought about her mother, about her family, about the smoke, about the feast. She walked and watched the mountaintop like it was speaking to her, like she was listening to it. A voice then called out that she recognized—and yet she kept walking. It was a man and he said a word over and over, calm but purposeful. The voice was from behind her but she didn't turn around. She walked on the highway.

"Alex," Hayden said. He was running towards her, Sara in his arms, Caleb holding his free hand. Alex looked at these people and knew who they were and yet required a moment to comprehend that this was *her* family, that Hayden's expression was grimaced. She knew that there was something to say and her mouth opened.

"Hayden," she said, first slowly, answering a question. Then, "Hayden," she nearly yelled, looking around, unsure where she was.

"Are you okay?" he asked.

"I think so," she looked around, inspected her hands and

arms. "What's going on?"

Hayden shook his head, "I don't know. I just found myself walking. But then I heard something break, like a window smashing. Sara and Caleb were wandering around the grounds just outside the house. I grabbed them and looked for you."

Sara reached out for her mother and Alex abided, relishing in the affection, the need to be held. She then realized, "My wine." Her hands were empty. She looked around the ground, first by her feet and then down the highway. Shards of glass reflected the waning sun a hundred meters down the road.

"Let's get back." Hayden said, pulling Caleb with him. As they approached the cabin, that once enticing smoke was now choking, catching in the back of each person's throat. The barbecue lid was open and the chicken thighs were blackened embers above ashen white coals. Caleb groaned and asked what happened, reminding people of how hungry he was. Hayden assured him that there was plenty more meat in the not-so-frozen freezer that needed to be used up. He then recommended that the kids play inside as the mosquitoes were getting irritating. Alex agreed and took them in, Caleb's mood improving once informed that he could play games on the computer. Sara hurriedly followed him up the stairs and Alex implored Caleb to let his little sister play as well. Alex didn't want to leave them alone but she needed to speak with Hayden. She left the patio door open, one ear to the loft as Hayden placed steaks on the sizzling grill. She waited for him to look at her, to say something, but upon making eye contact, Hayden only shook his head and said, "I don't know."

"They're fine?"

"I think so. Sara doesn't have a clue, of course. Caleb knows we're scared."

"Where were they when you found them?"

"Just down there, in the ferns."

"By the lake?"

"Not really. I don't know. I don't know where they were going."

Alex looked back inside, worried about that staircase, imagining Sara plunging down without a word spoken. She said, "I thought we'd be safe here," her words cracked. "But it's like back at home. When I cut myself. When we were on the highway."

Hayden was reluctant to reply. He closed the lid to the barbecue, looked at Alex and grabbed one hand. "How long do you want to stay?"

Alex shook her head.

Hayden added, "When the time comes, we should drive north."

"We have to give my mom a chance to come back."

After a protracted pause, Hayden nodded twice, not saying a word in accompaniment.

"They drove away," Alex said, "They could come back."

"I know. But I no longer feel at all safe here."

"It's not the same as the other places. We haven't seen any bodies."

"I fear we're still too close. That we should head north."

"After all we've been through just to get here, I can't leave yet. Not so soon."

"I know."

"We have to give them a chance to get back here."

Hayden nodded, eyes on the grill.

Alex was exhausted; their pre-dawn escape from Mount

Baker felt days in the past—days without sleep, without pause. Sara asked about Barbara while being tucked into bed. Before Alex could think of a suitable reply, Caleb said that she was gone and wasn't coming back. Alex thought of snapping back at him, telling him to shut up, but she couldn't get out a single word, instead staring at her son as he rested on his side, back towards her. Sara asked where Barbara had gone and Alex admitted that she didn't know. "Maybe tomorrow Nan will come back," was the most she could say. Caleb didn't refute anything and didn't rustle. Alex imagined him awaiting his mother's reprimand with open eyes, facing the wall. Alex lingered and watched, expecting him to roll over. She told them both that she loved them and locked the door.

"The kids should be safe," Alex said as she rested on the bed beside Hayden, thankful that he was beside her, that he wasn't going anywhere. Her eyes were sore but she was reluctant to close them, instead staring at a painting of a galloping horse that hung above the dresser across the room. In the pale, moonlit darkness, only a vague silhouette of the stallion's proud stride and stature could be discerned. Under the light of day, a mountainous wildflower vista emerged in the background. The thoroughbred sprinted untethered in an immaculate, unspoiled world. Alex found most of her mother's artwork distasteful; this one was the very worst.

"I can't sleep," Hayden said while sitting up, as if prodded. Alex thought she might have said something to annoy him. "I'm just going to sit out on the deck. I'll be fine." He kissed her cheek. "If we're going to stay here for a while, we can't be living our entire lives inside."

Alex didn't want him to go but didn't request that he stay. She didn't think she could fall asleep alone in her mother's bed, staring at the awful, trite painting. She closed her eyes and visualized the smoke from the barbeque casting the forest in an ochre fog. She walked along the fallen cedar needles in her bare feet, a glass of wine still in one hand. Sara called her over towards the deck, her arms waving through the mist. Alex wanted to hurry but approached with the same deliberate, almost lumbering steps. "What is it?" she asked, and Sara pointed towards the planter. There was that spider from last year. Its legs formed a circle the size of Alex's palm and she knelt down, wary not to spill any of her drink. Sara asked if that was the one she let live and Alex nodded. *The one she let live*, for she was a fair and (usually) benevolent god.

Hayden woke her up with a pair of gentle prods to her shoulder. She had to come outside. He offered no specifics and led the way out of the room.

As she descended the stairs, she expected the windows to flash. Hayden opened the door and waved her along with whispered words. The sky remained dark. She stepped out onto the patio, surprised by the coolness of the air, how it pricked her skin. "What?" she asked, wishing she had a blanket.

"Get your shoes on. We're going down to the lake."

"Why?"

"You have to see this. Trust me. It'll just be a minute."

"But what about—"

"They'll be fine. You locked the door. Like I said, you need to see this."

Alex no longer cared about the cold. She followed Hayden down a murky, mulch path, the lake water rippling ashen blue between the black trunks of trees. "Are you sure I want to see this?"

"Trust me." Pebbles clattered under Hayden's shoes as he

stepped onto the beach and pointed up towards the sky.

Alex said. "There's no flashing."

"I know. But look."

Alex looked. A crescent moon hung above the black ridge of the mountaintops and reflected against the splattering surface. The night sky was an ocean of innumerable stars, with depth and color so grandiose that it granted onlookers just the tiniest hint of how small we were in relation to the rest of the cosmos. Alex used to come down to the beach at night and lie on her back while stoned, admiring these details that were impossible to observe in the city. And she was about to tell this to Hayden: that this was nothing new, that he'd spent too much time in Vancouver. She'd begun to shake her head, ready to scoff. But then she saw something else, something new. There was a strand of light, a single silk thread across the sky, linear and unbroken, twinkling like the rest of the heavens. As she traced its length with her eyes, she caught sight of another strand, parallel to the first, gently arching with the curvature of the Earth. She then realized that there were four. Every time she noticed another streak, seconds later she'd discover even more, each spanning east to west, lines of latitude etched into the night sky. They had color, an iridescent spectrum of orange to green. She couldn't tell if they were changing or if her eyes were playing tricks on her.

"I've counted more than twenty." Hayden said as if asked.

Alex shook her head slowly, eyes transfixed on the sky.

"Look," Hayden pointed upwards and pulled Alex close so that her cheek pressed against his shoulder, directing her attention with the tip of his outstretched finger. "Right there, can you see it?"

"See what?"

"One's being made. Right there. Look."

Alex saw stars and those strands of twilight and then what seemed to be an especially bright star, a teardrop, its pointed end outlining another twinkling streak that crossed over the jagged mountaintop in behind her. It glided with the speed of a distant airplane, easy to follow once spotted. Alex wrapped an arm around Hayden's waist to pull him in closer. "What the fuck?" was all Alex could think of saying—because she needed to say something. She watched that interstellar tadpole glide without sound, imagining the entire world being trapped within a spider's web. A heavy sense of despair overwhelmed her, a feeling she hadn't experienced since that first night at Brent and Gillian's.

She asked, "Aren't you scared?"

"I don't know what I'm feeling right now."

"What are you thinking?"

"About what Simar said."

"You feel like an ant."

"I feel like an ant."

Alex looked back towards the cabin, its frame nearly indistinguishable in the darkness from the surrounding forest. She thought of Caleb and Sara, asleep and blissfully oblivious to this new world that they were inheriting.

Hayden said: "We should go tomorrow."

"You need to give me more time."

"This doesn't feel safe. We should go north."

"I can't leave yet. We just got here."

"Then what? When do we go?"

Alex looked up, unable to distinguish which of those iridescent fibers was the one she witnessed being traced into existence. "Give me one more day. Just one. I need to give them a chance."

"Okay. One more day. But if they don't return tomorrow, then we go first thing the following morning."

"You're talking as if you know they won't come back."

Hayden didn't answer. Then: "One day."

As soon as Alex woke up—before she checked on Caleb and Sara—she looked out the window to the clear sky of dawn. She saw only the wispy haze of high clouds between the feather-sharp peaks of trees. She left Hayden in bed and unlocked the guest room with the pointed tip of a safety pin, careful not to awake either of the kids as the door opened with a groaning squeal. She traipsed down the path to the lakeshore, the gravel and mulch covered in a cushioned bed of rusty needles. Back on the beach, the sun had not yet risen above the eastern mountains and the entire valley was lit without definition, without contrast. No matter how long she stared up to the heavens, there was no sign of those lines from the previous night. A lone crow sailed past, requiring only a pair of expeditious thrusts from its wings to keep it afloat above the water. The bird seemed determined to make it across to the opposite shore and Alex wondered if it could traverse that distance—almost five kilometers—without resting. If not, at which point would it decide to turn back? Or was it destined to lurch into the waters and drown, far from either shore, far from any witnesses?

Hayden told Alex of his plan to take Kevin's truck and visit the other houses along the east shore of the lake. Not even five minutes had passed since he'd descended the stairs from the bedroom and already he wanted to leave. Hayden said that he couldn't sit around the house all day just waiting. He might find others—people who could know the whereabouts of Barbara and Kevin. Alex didn't feel comfortable with any aspect of his proposal but it was this last point, that faint possibility, which allowed her to concede. Her mother had lived here for more than twenty years. Everyone knew everyone. "She might even be staying at one of their houses," Hayden added.

It sounded desperate. She'd already agreed but was still wary. "Just be quick." She repeated. "Even if you find people, don't stay away for long."

It felt like Hayden was putting on his shoes and coat within seconds of the conversation. Caleb then followed. Alex asked what he was doing and he assured her that Dad had given permission.

"Like hell he did."

"Actually," Hayden piped up, "he's right."

Alex wanted to tell him off. "What the—"

"There's no point him getting bored around here. He wanted to come. And you know, I want him to come."

"We'll be quick, Mom." Caleb assured. It sounded rehearsed.

Alex pulled Hayden close and whispered: "Are you fucking crazy?"

"He's not going on his own. He's with me."

"But you don't know what you're going to find?"

Hayden sighed. "It's not going to be any worse than what he's already seen. We're not going far. He wants to come. He can't just be cooped up inside these cabins forever."

Alex mulled her next words but Hayden took this as a sign of acceptance. He kissed her on the cheek and started walking away.

She pulled him back in. "Don't tell him about what we saw last night."

Hayden's eyebrows furrowed and his lips rounded, ready to ask, "*Why?*" He shook his head, shrugged, and nodded once. "Okay then. We won't be long. Promise."

Sara asked Alex to tell her a story. "A spooky story," she then added for clarification. This had been Sara's game for the last six months: requesting impromptu flash-fiction at any time, without warning. And to Sara, all tales could be divided into two mutually exclusive categories: funny and spooky. As Alex sighed, not feeling the inspiration to make up a children's story at that time, she then realized that this was the first time Sara had made such a request in days. Since they left Vancouver. Alex then chuckled, awash in a fleeting sense of relief, and kissed Sara in that mop of twisted hair. "Tell me a spooky story!" Sara repeated, not appreciating her mother's seeming disobedience.

"Okay then," Alex said, "But I'd rather make it a funny story."

"A funny story," Sara said, gleefully accepting her mother's deal.

Alex sat cross-legged on the forest floor, the stretch-mark streaks of a tree's trunk inches from her eyes. The shimmering waters of Kootenay Lake were out of focus, straight ahead, where the shrubs and arachnid-roots of the trees gave way to stones and pebbles. She felt grit between her fingers and lifted them up, her digits covered in dirt that crumbled from her skin as she ran them over her palm. She blinked as if awakening and yet was sure that she hadn't been sleeping. She looked around and saw the steep triangle roof of her mother's cabin up the gentle slope of the shore. Alex turned her neck from side to side—too complacent to stand—looking for anyone else, but there was no one. With each breath, she smelled that tart aroma of pine needles. She then noticed that her feet were bare, covered in dirt and small pebbles that had adhered themselves to the soiled bottoms. Her first thoughts were to wonder how she got here, unable to remember walking to this exact spot. She took another deep breath and felt that very first pang of concern. *How did I get here?*

She then thought: *Where is Sara?*

Alex stood, looking for any signs of movement. "Sara," Alex called out and her words vanished into the trees and open sky. "Sara?" Hearing no reply, Alex hesitated with where to go. She couldn't recall how she got here. It was like she'd been sleepwalking. She hurried towards the lake, wincing as her feet pressed upon the jagged rocks. She didn't want to, but it was an obvious place to look. She took two steps into the glacial cold water, calling out her daughter's name, desperate to hear a response. The cold crept up her ankles and shins as if by osmosis and she took another further step out, the water now licking each knee. She called out again and again, pausing mere seconds in between to hear any possible response. No one replied and no one floated in the water. She charged back onto the beach, the entire world around her too expansive. There was no one place to start searching. So, she yelled. She could already imagine Sara walking without thought through the forest. Up the mountain. Off a ridge. Into the lake. She remembered that girl with the smooth trimmed black hair, neck back and mouth open, teeth exposed, gaping holes where there were once eyes. "No," she said aloud, not letting herself succumb to those thoughts, "Not yet," she said because she could, because no one else was around to hear her. She ran up towards the cabin. The front door was open. Her feet slid on the linoleum and she nearly tumbled to the floor, still calling Sara's name. Alex required less than a minute to search every room before returning to the deck, knowing that every second was precious. Every second counts. She called out shriller than before, her voice breaking, her breaths quivering and dividing her daughter's name into abbreviated bursts. She looked back and forth through the stalks of tree trunks, wishing that Hayden was here, that there was someone else to help her. She was going to run up towards the road. There was no time for shoes and she sprinted off from the deck. And she heard a voice. She stopped and tried to listen above her heaving breaths.

It was a girl. Calling for her mother. It was Sara. It was surely Sara and her voice came from up the hill, towards the highway. Alex called back, telling her that she was coming. And when she saw her daughter's coils of amber blonde hair contrasting the malt bark of cedar trees, when she saw the girl turn to face her with open eyes and a gaping mouth—when she knew that Sara was alive and unhurt—Alex let herself cry. She picked up Sara, the girl barefoot and covered in ashen dirt, and kissed her before running hands down her arms, legs, back, head. She asked, "Are you okay?" Sara nodded and cried and shook her head. Alex took her back into the cabin, telling her that she was going to be fine. She tried to put her down on the sofa, to let her go for only a few seconds in order to get a wet cloth with warm water, but Sara would not unwrap her arms and legs. Alex sat down, dirt and needles and pebbles and all, pulling Sara in closer.

The door opened and before Alex could question who it might be, Hayden entered. His expression made it clear that she would not have the time to explain to him what had happened with Sara. There was no time for anything. "I think we should go," were his first words, expressed without concern for the fact that the kids were listening. "I think we should pack the essentials, siphon gas from Kevin's truck, and go."

Caleb stood behind his father, awaiting orders. Alex looked at him and then to Hayden. She asked, "What happened?"

"We saw dead people," Caleb said, his tone fearless, almost excited. "They were shot."

Alex mumbled out a stuttered, "What?"

"Caleb, please." Hayden ushered him along towards his room. "Go pack your things. And help Sara do the same."

"Hayden?" Alex began, angry that he was giving her no room for dissent and scared with what was being alluded to. She intended to say more but left it at the one word, a question, almost begging.

He took her by the shoulder and directed her to the deck, looking around the corner of the house before starting. "Shit, Alex. I think it's those men, those men we saw on the highway yesterday. I think they've been through here."

"What happened? What's Caleb talking about?"

"We stopped into a few cabins along the highway but they were all locked or empty. I didn't want to go looting with Caleb so we drove up to Gray Creek. And there we found a house just off the road with the front door open. But there was something different. There were several cars parked in front. More than you'd expect to see. So, we went in and there were bodies, at least five, six, maybe seven. But this was different.

They had gunshot wounds. Fucking Caleb was standing right with me. They were all shot in the head, others also in the chest and legs. I told Caleb to leave and on the way out I saw another body just beside the house, between a couple of cars. It was a woman. She was," Hayden stalled, troubled. "She was young, like twenty or thirty. She was on the ground," Hayden shook his head, not wanting to say it. "I think she was raped. Her jeans were pulled down to her knees and she was face down in the gravel. Caleb didn't see that. He started coming so I got out of there. Told him to get in the truck and go." Hayden looked back towards the highway. "Maybe the survivors were all in one spot and those men robbed them or? I don't know. I don't know why anyone would do that. We've seen a lot. But never in all these last days did we see people shot. Not raped. This was so very different."

"Did you recognize any of the people—"

"No, no. Your mom and Kevin weren't there. I'm sure of that much. Look, I know we said we could stay until tomorrow but we need to get going. This place isn't safe."

Hayden sounded conciliatory but Alex felt that she was being hemmed in, cornered. She slowly shook her head and said, "I can't leave just yet. We've hardly been here for twenty-four hours."

"And your son and I saw just saw a mass execution."

"It wasn't my idea for him to tag along."

"It's not about what he saw. It's about what happened."

"We've seen a lot of terrible shit, Hayden."

"This is different. If you saw that woman, you'd know what I mean." Hayden's red eyes glistened. "I just thought about you when I saw her."

Alex wanted more time to think. This all just came at her

so quickly and without consultation. Her opinion was not worth investigating. She looked back towards the lake and that tree in front of which she had found herself sitting. She hadn't even had a chance to tell him. She just wanted a moment to think but Hayden was stoked on adrenaline.

He said, "We need to go. Now."

"You don't call the shots, Hayden."

"Fuck!" He swore up to the sky. Alex stepped back, afraid from the look in his eyes. He continued, "Why does everything have to be a fucking power struggle with you? We need to go. That's it."

"And I just want to think. Can't I have a fucking minute to think?"

"No. You can't actually."

"You're not the fucking boss of this family. You don't just make orders for us all like this."

"And what the fuck happened back in Vancouver? When you called me up at the university? Told me that we had to go? You sure sounded like you were giving orders back then."

"I saved your fucking life back then," Alex was so angry that she didn't care that Caleb and Sara were watching from inside, standing at the opposite side of the living room, listening.

"And I'm trying to save your life, as well. But if you don't want to go," Hayden stopped, lips twitching, grimacing. "Maybe I'll just leave right now with the kids. You can find your own fucking way out of here. Or stay, for all I fucking care."

"Don't you dare talk of taking the kids."

"That's what you said to me at the university! Remember?" Hayden looked inside towards Caleb and Sara, expecting them to scurry away out of sight. But Caleb stood his ground by the open door, making eye contact with his father, Sara in behind. Hayden's chest heaved, his breaths billowing, shaking his head and resisting the urge to say another word with haste. He then looked at Alex. "Barbara is not coming back. The sooner you accept that, the better."

There was so much that Alex wanted to say at that moment. She wanted to curse at him, tell him that she should have left him at the university, that she didn't love him anymore, that she didn't need him. But instead she cried, her lips and lungs quivering, her eyes caught on her children watching this all from across the deck. They'd seen unimaginable horrors over these last days but never before had they witnessed their parents fight quite like this. Never before had Alex felt such abhorrence towards the man that she'd married. She didn't care that Caleb was listening. She said, "I fucking hate you."

Hayden shrugged, dismissive. "Right now, I don't care."

"I'm giving my mother a chance to come home."

"We're leaving tonight. And until then, we stay inside with the generator off. Nothing to warrant any attention." Hayden didn't give Alex the time to reply, instead returning inside, shutting the door behind him. She could hear him instruct Sara and Caleb to go to their room. Alex stayed on the deck, letting her heart and breaths settle, knowing that soon enough she would regret so much of what she'd said.

Her knees were beneath the water. Alex looked down and her lower legs seemed an inches' long deformation beneath the rippled surface. She could feel the rocks beneath her bare feet, a jagged pebble pushing into the crook under her right big toe. The sky was a lavender sheet with pinholes of starlight breaking through. She turned around and nearly fell, her feet numb and sliding on the gelatinous, wooly slick that coated the submerged rocks. She took a step and realized how frigid the lake was. The shore was still a few lumbering paces away. She remembered sitting in the house. She remembered sitting on the couch, looking out the window towards the lake that she was now standing in. She remembered the argument with Hayden, neither saying another word to each other afterwards. She remembered wanting to apologize, wanting to tell him that she had gone too far. But she waited for him to apologize first. She didn't think he ever did. She couldn't remember.

A twinkling burst of light caught her eye, high above the dark peaks of the mountains across the shore. Another thread of luminous silk was sketched across the heavens, reflecting the embers of the already set sun. She then noticed dozens of others, glimmering into existence with the onset of stars. Alex didn't admire the scale of what she was witnessing and she didn't fear her insignificant place in it either. She traced these lines from mountaintop to mountaintop with a slow and controlled arc of her neck.

She took a step and her foot slid forward. The water enveloped her, the world now dark and without room to breathe. Her hands slapped down desperate on the rocks and Alex scrambled, feeling awoken, lucid, and stood up, the lake bitterly cold. She took awkward, lunging steps back towards the beach, her hands soon clutching warm pebbles as she crawled onto dry land. She stood up and called out first for Hayden, then Caleb, then Sara. Waiting mere seconds, she repeated their names, her bare feet picking up sand and fallen needles with each step towards the cabin. The patio door was wide open but inside the house was empty. Shivering from the water that dripped from her chin and ears, she lingered only long enough to grab a towel and a pair of sandals. Back on the deck, she screamed the names in the same order. Hayden. Caleb. Sara. And someone yelled back. She was sure that it was Caleb. Calling out his name again, the boy replied from the boathouse and his shadowy figure emerged from behind the structure, waving and calling her Mommy, not Mom. She hugged him and he seemed repulsed by her sodden clothes.

He asked, "Where were you?"

"In the lake—it doesn't matter. I'm fine. What were you doing?"

He seemed confused to be asked such a thing, as if he hadn't thought about it already. Slowly, he answered: "I don't know."

"Do you know where Dad is? Where Sara is?"

Caleb shook his head.

"Come with me," Alex grabbed him by the hand and pulled him back towards the cabin. "Hayden? Sara? I've got Caleb!" Finding her son—and with such swiftness—made her hopeful. She would find Sara. She would find Hayden. She just didn't know where to look.

"Mom?" Caleb asked once back by the cabin. She vacillated over which direction to search next, desperate for a reply. "What's going on? I don't remember going down there."

"We just have to find Dad. And Sara."

"Where are they?"

"That's what I'm trying to figure out. But I'm not letting you out of my sight. Come," she pulled him up the driveway towards the highway, calling out Hayden's and Sara's names. Caleb joined in seconds later, his voice trembling at the end of each.

"*Please, please, please,*" Alex muttered under her breath, not wanting Caleb to hear and yet needing to say something. "Hayden? Sara?" When she reached the highway, the day's heat still emanated from the asphalt even though the adjacent forests were dark, the details in between the tall spires of trees vanishing. Above the points of trees, the sky appeared entrapped in a net of arcing lines. It was unavoidable. Caleb's neck craned upwards and he stopped moving.

"What is that?" he asked.

Alex wished that she could for once give her children an answer. Something definite. Something that would quell their concerns, their anxiety. She knelt down and kissed him in the hair above his ear. "I'm sorry, Caleb. I don't know. I just don't know."

It was as if for the moment Caleb had forgotten that his father and sister were missing. He stood still, eyes tracing back and forth, awestruck. Alex thought he might ask another question—his mouth was open, lips twitching to pronounce that first sound—but they then closed shut and he swallowed.

"I'm sorry," Alex said again, not knowing what else to say. She sniffled, unable to withhold a tear from heaving over the ridge of her eyelids. "I'm so sorry." She had forty years of life before this. She had her childhood, her adolescence, her twenties, her thirties all before this moment. Caleb had nine years. It wasn't fair for him to witness so many things beyond his—or anyone's—comprehension.

Hayden's voice cut through Caleb's deliberate, heavy breaths. He was behind them, emerging from the forest and sprinting as soon as he'd cleared the uneven underbrush. Alex stood, heaving up Caleb in her arms so that they could all embrace with their eyes level. He kissed them both before looking around. His next words were obvious: "Where's Sara?"

Alex shook her head, tears down each cheek, "I just found Caleb a minute ago, down by the boathouse."

"Where were you?"

"I was in the lake," she said, "Just knee deep. You?"

"In the forest, just up the mountain. I don't know—" Hayden shook his head, changing the topic. "We have to find Sara. We should split up. We can meet up at the house."

"I don't want to split up anymore." Alex said, "I don't know what's going to happen."

"We have to cover ground. We have to move fast. I'll go down to the lake. Caleb, you search Nan's property, and Alex, why don't you stay along the highway?"

"Not Caleb. We can't leave him on his own."

"We need everyone we can get. We need him. We need you," Hayden said to his son, gripping his shoulder and kissing him on the forehead. "Just go." Hayden took Caleb with him back towards the driveway, leaving Alex alone on the road. Hayden yelled Sara's name and Caleb repeated. Alex looked along both directions of the highway, watching her son and husband exit, it feeling unfair that Hayden would take Caleb away from her so quickly. They vanished back into the darkness between the trees, their voices still echoing. Alex turned, jogged down the road and joined in. Each time she hollered, she paused for just a few seconds, her breaths and scraping footsteps filling the void in between. She imagined how wonderful it would feel to hear her daughter's reply. To call out for her mother. It would happen. She just couldn't give up. It would happen.

Hayden left the generator running and every light in the cabin was on, the windows bright squares, rectangles and triangles in the darkness, a Cheshire cat grin. The building would be a beacon, easily visible from the highway. Alex swung her flashlight beam around, no longer having the will to call out Sara's name every few seconds. For those first few hours, Alex felt that she was on the edge of breaking down each time she repeated herself, the very act of vocalizing her daughter's name chipping away at her own defenses. Now she was deliberate and careful. Her voice was haggard, her vocal chords scraping the bottom of a dry barrel. She'd tripped on a serpentine tree root and now with every step something seemed to pinch from within her right knee. Shining her light on the wound, blood trickled out from a rash of small punctures, dark lines trailing down to her ankles. But it felt selfish to linger on her own injuries, shining the light back towards the forest around her, the beam flashing against nearby trunks like a strobe.

Impatient for the sun to rise, Alex reclined with her back against the patio door, legs out straight on the wooden deck. Hayden sat beside her underneath a knitted quilt. Alex didn't need any sleep. She just needed daylight. It was the darkness that kept her from searching any further. Hayden promised that he would stay out with her until dawn and it made her angry when she'd find his eyes closing shut, a creaking snore sneaking in with each unconscious breath. No matter the exhaustion, it seemed cruel that he could sleep while their daughter was out there. Somewhere. Alive but alone. Then Alex would open her eyes and realize that she'd been dreaming, unsure if it had been mere seconds or minutes or more. A slurping inhale and clearing of the throat announced Hayden's awakening. He looked at Alex and kissed her on the cheek. She thought he was going to say something but he instead stood up and leaned over the railing.

"I'm sorry," Alex said, "about earlier today. About the things I said. I'm sorry."

"We don't need to talk about this now. It doesn't matter what we said. It's all meaningless now."

"But I really am sorry."

Hayden nodded, looking up towards the iridescent web arching above the clouds. "I'm also sorry. I was scared. I'm still scared." She couldn't see his expression but Alex heard him sniffle. She imagined the tears down one cheek, then another. He seemed content to stand, looking towards the placid lake, a pool of mercury reflecting the moon. Alex closed her eyes and thought about Sara, alone in the forest, too far from anyone for them to hear her whimpers. That was the best-case scenario.

"When you go out looking in the morning," Hayden added, talking into the forest, "make sure you take a knife with you. Those people might be out there still. The ones with the guns. You need to be able to protect yourself. There are Swiss army knives in one of the kitchen drawers. Take one with you."

"I'm so sorry, Hayden."

"You don't need to—"

"No, you don't know. You don't know why I'm so sorry."

"Please, Alex. There's no point—"

"I lost her earlier today, while you were out with Caleb. This happened in the morning. I came to sitting in front of a tree. And I found Sara up by the highway. It was just like before. I'm sorry. I wanted to tell you. I did."

Hayden faced Alex, head cocked. "This happened while I was gone?"

"Yes. But I found her. And I was going to tell you. But you came home—"

"It happened earlier and you didn't tell me?"

Alex shook her head. "It didn't happen to you and Caleb?"

"No. And if it did I would have told you."

"I'm sorry, Hayden."

"Why didn't you fucking tell me?" He almost yelled.

"You came home and didn't give me a chance. You jumped straight into the need to get going right there and then and—"

"And we should have fucking gone. Right then. We should have gotten the fuck out of here."

"I didn't know it was going to happen again. I don't even know what's happening. What's real or not. I thought we could—"

"What are we doing?"

"I'm sorry."

"You," Hayden said, shaking his head as if disagreeing with what was being said. Tears ran down his cheeks with a twisting sneer. "You," he repeated, his next words either too obvious or too dangerous to speak.

"I'm going to find her, Hayden."

"You did this."

"Don't you fucking say that."

"If we left when I said—"

"Shut the fuck up. Shut the fuck up. Don't you fucking put this all on me."

Hayden couldn't look at Alex, instead walking to the far end of the deck, hunched over the railing, muttering.

"I'm going to find her, Hayden." Alex said, her voice trembling, pleading, desperate. "I'm going to find her."

The approaching sunrise lit the eastern clouds violet, bright enough to wash away most of the celestial webbing that entwined the Earth. Within minutes, all traces of it would be gone. Alex wanted to jog but her legs limped, her knees locked, and so she plodded, leaning forward with each step, those first hints of dawn giving her another boost. She had a system now. After calling Sara's name she'd count to sixty, one second for each pair of steps, and then repeat. She entered every cabin or house that she passed, jiggling locks and pounding on single-paned windows if the doors wouldn't budge. Every shed, every garage, she rattled the doors and called out Sara's name. And each time the highway swung tight against the edge of the lake and afforded her an unobstructed panorama of the water, she stopped to inspect the rolling waves and distant, silent whitecaps. If Sara was out there, then she needed to know. When she yelled out above the valley, her voice vanished into the expanse. No matter how loud she was, it felt that she was too quiet, too inconsequential. When she thought of sitting and crying, she called out again and counted aloud to sixty.

She didn't tell Hayden when she left. They didn't say another word after her admission. Caleb either slept through their argument or stayed in his room. Once there was enough light to see her steps, Alex continued her search. If she began to think about what would happen should she not find Sara, Alex would call out her name again and count louder than before. There was no time for such thoughts. Every second counts.

The sun burst over the peaks of the eastern mountains, its rays heralding the remorseless passage of time. It was dusk when Sara vanished. The highway veered around a tight ridge and sunlight warmed her face. She'd been walking for at least two hours. She recalled the last words she'd said to Hayden. She was going to find Sara. She said these words and yet Alex didn't know if she was genuine. Standing along the yellow center line of a road several kilometers away from where she started, it felt like a lie, the sort of thing she'd told her children countless times over the years. *Everything is going to be okay.* Just because she could—and because no one could hear her—Alex began repeating that line: "I'm going to find Sara. Trust me. I'm going to find her. I'm going to find her. Trust me. I'm going to find her." She was mocking herself with her own words. What was the point in walking any further? Just because she could search, did it mean that she was getting any closer?

Alex sat down on the pavement; it was cool to the touch. She thought to herself: *I'm not giving up.* She said to the highway: "I'm not giving up on you, Sara. I'm not giving up." She began to cry and didn't care. She said it again: "I'm not going to give up on you, Sara. I'm not going to give up." She looked down, a fallen tear marking the dusty asphalt black, "I'm going to find you." And for the first time since Alex awakened from her daze, knee deep in Kootenay Lake, she followed through with the entire thought: My daughter might be dead.

What she first assumed to be the rustle of wind proved to be an approaching vehicle, the unseen engine coughing and accelerating. It might have been Hayden. He had found Sara and was driving to find Alex. Although reluctant, this fantastical thought took precedence upon all others. She knew that there were many possibilities but Alex didn't ponder them. She stood up, certain that the automobile was coming from behind. The direction of the cabin. Her heart raced. If she saw Sara's face peering over the lip of the windshield, then Alex would agree to go to any destination that Hayden requested. Nothing else mattered. She took slow steps, wanting to run but tempering that desire, waiting for the car to appear around the corner.

Hoping to see the minivan. Kevin's faded black truck.

A white pickup straddled the centerline of the highway. Even if she knew what to do, there was no way she could hide without being noticed. She stood, hands limp and pinching her jeans at each thigh. She could distinguish only a single figure behind the wheel. Her right foot skittered, tempted to run. It was a man. He wore a black baseball cap. The truck slowed and the Oakland Raiders logo was unmistakable. His eyes followed hers, a dimpled smile widening and revealing those wide, white teeth. She backed towards the edge of the road, the gravel that framed the asphalt giving way to tall grasses that plummeted to the water below—a ten, maybe twenty-meter drop. The truck stopped in the opposite lane and the passenger window lowered. The man leaned with one hand on the adjacent seat to project his voice out from the opening: "Well, you look familiar, don't you?"

Alex swallowed. She couldn't jump into the water but figured she might scamper down the embankment. She inspected the drop behind her, knowing that her eyes were betraying any attempts at being inconspicuous.

He said, "Why don't you come in with me?"

She shook her head.

"It's not a choice." He opened the door to reveal his rifle on the passenger's seat, one hand gripping the chamber. "Get in."

"I'm looking for my daughter—"

"Get the fuck in."

Alex swallowed, glancing back, figuring it was already too late to flee.

He added, "Go down there and I'll just shoot you."

"Please, I'm begging you—"

He picked up the rifle and pointed the barrel at her chest. "You have five seconds."

It was one thing to see a gun slung over his shoulder or gripped on an empty seat. But eying the black circular opening, unambiguously aimed at her chest from mere feet away, caused her knees to twitch, her stomach to slither. He started counting, so similar in tone and speed to how she'd announce an impending time-out for Sara. She took a step forward, holding out both hands as if she might shield herself from a bullet with her palms. He stopped counting and pulled the rifle to his side, vacating the passenger seat, its leather cracked like dried scabs, seams of fabric exposed. Alex slid onto the right side, maximizing her distance from the man.

"Close the door," he ordered. The fingers of his right hand dangled over the wooden butt of the rifle. She closed the door. "Smart woman," he said, shifting into drive and depressing the gas. Alex watched the embankment drift away, wondering if she could still open the door and tumble out, furious that she did nothing when she had the chance, that she just stood in the middle of the highway deluded by the fantasy that it was Hayden and that he'd found Sara.

"Where's your husband?"

"Please—"

"Where's your fucking husband?"

"He's back at the cabin."

"Where was it he said you were all going? Moyie Lake?"

"We didn't have enough gas."

"Shut the fuck up. Where is the place you're staying at?"

"It's back a while. I don't know how far. Please, you have to listen. I've lost my daughter. She's only three. She walked off and I can't find her." Tears flooded down each cheek and

Alex made no attempt to control them. "I don't care what you guys are doing, I just need to find her." She looked at him, expecting him to at least interrupt if not reply. If anything, he seemed to grin. She asked, "Do you," her lungs heaved. She tried again: "Do you have a child?"

"Why the fuck do you think I'd give a shit about anything?"

"Don't you have a nephew? Or a niece?"

"You don't fucking get it, do you? You know how many dead people I've seen in these last few days? How many dead kids? Your daughter means nothing to me. I don't give a shit."

Alex coughed, sputtering out tears, feeling herself lose control. "How can you say that? After all you must have gone through, how can you say that?"

"After what we've been through, none of that shit matters."

The truck's rattling engine whined as he took both lanes to maneuver the tight turns in the highway, every second hurtling her farther away from Hayden and Caleb. The asphalt blurred past. It was too late to flee. She did not heed Hayden's advice to take a knife with her. She had a pair of keys in her right jeans pocket, the ring protruding into her thigh. The man wasn't saying anything, seemingly content to drive in silence. When she felt that she could speak without her voice trembling, Alex asked: "What are you going to do with me?"

As if clearing his throat, he released a single, scratching chuckle. He then glanced over and said, "Simple." He said nothing else.

"Simple?"

"Simple. I'm going to fuck you."

Alex wanted to remain strong. She thought she could be stoic, no matter what he'd said. But she didn't expect such forthrightness. Like a switch being flicked, she was sick to her stomach, ready to throw up.

He laughed again, "I kinda like being so honest, you know? I can say whatever the fuck I want. You see? The first time I saw you, I wanted to fuck you. Don't know why I let you guys go. Moment of weakness, I guess. And no matter what you say or what you do, it's going to happen. You might be the last fucking woman I ever see, so I'm not going to waste this."

Alex hyperventilated. She had lost control. She sucked in gasps of air so quickly that she coughed.

The man shook his head. "I never said I was going to kill you. You might think that I'm fucking evil or something, but that's not it. What I am is a fucking survivor. And I don't know how much longer I'm going to survive for, so I don't see the point in putting up with any shit that pisses me off, you know? So, if I were you, I would get your fucking shit together right now—right fucking now—or else things are going to get really, really fucking ugly for you really, really fucking soon. Got it?"

Alex tried. She pursed her lips together, bent over, wrestling her lungs to inhale and exhale with a steady rhythm. She nodded, hoping it might buy her time, nodding and holding up a hand towards him. "Please," she eked out, unable to say more than a syllable between trembling breaths. "Please."

"Please, what?"

Alex shook her head, looking him in the eyes, desperate that such a momentary form of contact would be enough to keep him from doing anything too rash, too quickly.

He said, "I bet we're all going to be dead in the next week. I bet there will be no one left alive. Every single person on Earth. So, your daughter won't mean anything to anyone soon enough. I won't mean anything to anyone. You won't mean anything to anyone. We'll be fucking dead."

Alex nodded, said, "Okay," once and then twice, eyes focused on the road ahead. The man accelerated in the brief stretches between turns, nodding to himself, looking and smiling.

"That's better," he said.

"Okay," Alex repeated. A trio of black arrows on tangerine signs directed drivers to the right with caution. He slowed down.

"I thought you might be bitching the entire time."

"Okay," she nodded again, expressing this word with assurance. One last breath in. And then out. "Okay."

"I think you might actually—"

Alex swung her right fist, clutching the keys within so that the toothy spires jutted out between her fingers like a pair of talons. One key scraped against the man's temple while the other plunged into his cornea, his eyelids clenching down onto the metal as if to hold it in place. He screamed—a moment of disbelief too late—one hand clutching his right eye while the other reached out to push away Alex as she recoiled. The truck grumbled as it veered onto gravel, branches attacking and cracking against the driver-side window. The keys still projected out from her clenched fist. One was dry and dull, the other wet and glistening. This man was going to rape her. This man was going to kill her. She swung for his neck and both keys sunk into the soft but resistant flesh, the jagged teeth of each blade scraping against the webbing between her fingers before breaking through the man's skin and sinking in. Blood sprayed back into her face, her fingertips against a tap of warm water. The truck swiped the solid trunk of a tree, propelling both against the dash before rolling up against an embankment. Alex tumbled back into her seat and then into her door. Silent spurts of the man's blood covered her face, her arms, the windshield, her legs. The truck slowed to a halt in the middle of the highway, facing the lake. The engine idled. The man gargled through his cries, reaching out for Alex with slippery fingers that smeared down her forearms. She kicked him back against his door and he looked at her with just one eye, his mouth open, unable to say a word. His teeth were still white, square, immaculate. Her hands were empty. The keys were by her feet. Every half-second, another burst from between his fingers. She thought he might say something. She tried to pick up the keys but they fell through her grip, the metal wet, warm, slippery. He shook his head, tried to speak but only coughed. The truck shuddered and Alex sat still with her knees up on the seat, ready to kick him if he came after her. It might have been seconds. It might have been minutes. He leaned forward and his forehead hit the steering wheel, his hand falling, liquid spewing down onto the pedals. She could hear it splatter against the seat with each of his slowing heartbeats. A splash of water against pavement.

It wasn't until she climbed out and tried to stand that Alex realized how much her entire body trembled. Her legs stumbled. She held onto the vehicle, her hands daubing red prints along the white and rust. Opening the driver's door, the man tumbled back and onto the asphalt, his head cracking against the ground, an axe splitting wood. He bled, but was no longer erupting. She didn't say a word. Her breaths were hoarse, as if she had a lung infection. She climbed over him and pushed aside an inch-deep puddle of blood in his seat with her hands. She shifted into reverse but her foot slipped off the pedal. She tried again and the engine revved. She relished in that sound. Something familiar. Something else. Not those gurgling gasps. Those splattering gushes. The crisp thud of bone against pavement. As Alex drove back to the cabin, she watched the road through the blurred smears and streaks on the windshield. She didn't notice her soaking clothes. She couldn't see the splotches across her cheeks and forehead. But it was the sounds that wouldn't escape her. That wouldn't leave her.

"Jesus Christ," Hayden said as Alex took the first cautious step out. She didn't want to stumble, knowing her legs could give out at any moment. "Alex," he started, ready to ask a question, his words hanging.

"Where's Caleb?"

"What the fuck happened?"

She repeated with urgency. "Where's Caleb?"

"He's inside."

"Did you find Sara?" She reached out to the trunk of a cedar, holding onto its withered, feathery bark for support.

Hayden's mouth hung open, looking at his wife, afraid. "What happened to you?"

Alex repeated with force: "Did you find Sara?"

"No." Hayden seemed unwilling to let her come within reach. "Alex, what happened to you?"

"You didn't find Sara?"

"Alex, for fuck's sake, are you okay?"

She hung her head and slunk down to the ground, her back to the tree.

"Alex?"

"I couldn't find her."

Hayden knelt down, looking over her arms and legs. "Alex," he said slowly, she was a child needing reassurance.

"Whose blood is this?"

Alex replied to the ground. "That man."

"Which man?"

"With the Raider's cap."

"From before? With the rifle?"

She nodded.

"Did he," Hayden deliberated over the right word, but Alex shook her head.

"He was going to."

"But?"

"He didn't."

"What the fuck happened?"

Alex shook her head, "I couldn't find Sara."

"Was he alone?"

Alex nodded.

"Where is he?"

Alex shook her head.

He asked with disbelief, "Did you kill him?"

Alex cried, not able or willing to make eye contact with anyone.

Hayden's eyes traced her steps back from the vehicle. "Is that his truck?"

"Mom?" Caleb stood behind Hayden, startling him. Alex didn't seem to notice, her head cumbersome and heavy.

Hayden said, "Caleb, go back into the house, right now."

"What happened to Mom?"

"Caleb," Hayden stood, holding his son by the shoulders. "Go inside, get all your stuff and put it into Kevin's truck."

"Is Mom okay?"

"I'm helping her right now. Just go. Go."

Alex kept her head down, unable to look at her son,

unwilling to witness his reaction. Hayden repeated his instructions to Caleb and the boy listened, hurrying inside. Alex listened to his steps and inspected the fallen cedar needles between her legs. Hayden sat in front of her, his hand reaching out to cup her chin, pulling back at the last moment.

"Alex," he said, "What did he do to you?"

She sniffled but didn't reply and wouldn't look up.

"Did he—touch you?"

Alex shook her head. "He was going to."

"Did he talk about there being others?"

"I don't know."

"Alex," Hayden tried to look her in the eyes but she flinched and pushed him back. "Did you kill him?"

Slowly, she nodded. "I think so."

"Jesus Christ."

"He was going to rape me."

Hayden inched back, looking over the trickles and smears of blood in her jeans, in her shirt, bunches of hair that stuck together. "How? How did you do it?"

"I stabbed him with my keys."

"And you killed him?"

"I stabbed him in the eyes and then in the neck."

Hayden let those words sink in, unable to think, let alone reply. He wanted to stand. He wanted to step back. He sat still.

Alex looked up: "We have to find Sara."

"Where is he?"

"We have to find Sara."

Hayden stood, tried not to stagger, and strode towards the white truck, the driver side door open. A pair of red handprints marked the rusted hood. The seats were wet. A glazed burgundy hue stained the black plastic on the dash. The man's rifle pointed towards the back of the cab, the butt up in the air. "Jesus Christ, Alex."

"He told me that he was going to fuck me. Just like that. Like it was nothing."

"Where is he?"

"On the highway."

"How far from here?"

"I don't know. A few minutes."

"Are there others?"

"I don't know. I don't know if there are others. He was alone."

"We have to get out of here now. Right now."

"We have to find Sara."

"We have to go now. We'll take only the basics. We leave now."

"We have to find Sara."

Hayden looked up the driveway, towards the highway. "If those people who were with him find his body, they're going to find us. And they'll find this truck. You can see it from the highway. We have to go."

When Alex stood, Hayden stepped back. She could tell from the look on his face that each blotch of blood on her skin meant so much more to him now. She was a killer. He was scared of her. She stepped forward. "We can't leave without finding Sara."

"Alex, if those people come back, they will kill us all. No question. We have to go."

"We don't even know if there are others. He might be the last one."

"We can't take that risk. We've taken too many fucking

risks as it is."

She shook her head, fresh tears tracing clean lines down her skin. "You're going to leave her behind?"

"Don't say that," he took one tenuous step forward. "I think we have to be realistic, Alex."

"No, no, we have to find Sara. I said I was going to find her. I'm going to find her."

"Alex," Hayden held her shoulders, pulling her closer, tears blurring his vision. "She's not coming back."

She pushed at his chest, "Don't fucking say that."

"Alex—"

"Don't fucking say that. We have to find her. How can you say that? She's our little girl."

"Don't you fucking think this is easy for me. She's my girl too, Alex. She's my little girl. But we have to fucking go. We have to go now."

"Don't make me leave."

"Alex, she's gone. She's gone."

"She's not—"

"She's gone, Alex. We need to go."

"I said I was going to find her—"

"It doesn't matter what you said."

"I let her go—"

"No, no, no. Don't. We have to go now."

"She needs us."

"She's gone, Alex."

"We need to fucking find her." Alex pushed Hayden away, her expression casting blame. "I'm going to find her."

Hayden wiped his eyes and nose. He knew that Caleb was watching, that he was just around the corner. "No, you're not."

"You can't tell me what to do."

"We're going right now. Caleb and I. I'm not going to let him die."

"You don't know that she's dead."

"She's gone, Alex."

"You don't have the right to take Caleb with you."

"Rights? What are you talking about? What fucking rights? I'm taking him because I'm saving his life. I'm not going to let him die."

"You don't know that Sara is dead."

"Sara is dead. That's the truth."

"How can you say that?"

"Everyone is fucking dead. And we're all going to die if we stay here any longer."

"You sound just like him."

"What?"

Alex shook her head. "You sound like him."

Hayden dismissed her comment. "Caleb and I are going."

"And you're going to leave me here?"

"If you think we're going to stay any longer, yes."

"You're going to leave me here? After what just happened?"

"You're not thinking straight, Alex. We need to go. You need to come with us. We should have fucking left yesterday."

Alex gaped, looking at Hayden and then Caleb. Her son stood obedient beside the deck, holding a bag in one hand, terrified to come any closer. Terrified of her. Her legs buckled and she fell back to the ground.

Hayden reached out to Caleb, urging him over without words. When they gripped hands, Hayden said to Alex, his voice tender: "Every second counts, Alex. You know it's true. Every second counts."

PART
SIX

She looked at her fingernails. Hayden drove Kevin's truck without saying a word. Caleb watched out the passenger window, afraid to ask a single question. Alex sat in behind, her back against the side of the cab, legs across the seat, staring at her fingers. She only had a few minutes to wash her face and arms, to change her clothes. She'd run her hands under the tap and burrowed a bar of soap against them until the foam dribbled down white, not pink. And yet still every fingernail remained capped with a crescent of dried blood as dark as soil. It crept beneath her cuticles. Alex didn't know how many hours they would drive for. A destination was never mentioned. But for the entire journey, she would not be able to do away with these stains. So, she stared at them, making no attempt to ignore what she had done. She was alive because she'd killed a man. She was alive because of a tangle of random chances, choices that she'd made, quirks of character, pure and indifferent happenstance. Luck, Hayden called it with a tone that implied cold probability. Give enough people a hundred coins and eventually someone will flip all heads. If one thing had been different, she would be dead. If she still worked. If she hadn't cut herself. If Tricia never texted her. If she hadn't obsessed. If she was happy. If she hadn't turned on the radio. If she decided to turn left instead of right. If she stayed home. If she never stopped at the border. If she didn't keep that pair of keys in her pocket. If she'd swung just a little too low, too high, too far to the left or to the right. If she was anyone else aside from Alexandra Maclean. But now that indifferent luck had run out on her. She didn't have a choice. The previous one hundred events mattered not. She flipped the coin and it landed on tails.

When they passed the body of the man, he hadn't moved. His bloodied face beheld the sky, his expression calm, indifferent. Snapped branches of trees littered one lane towards a sharp turn. Not wanting Caleb to see any details of the scene, Hayden barely slowed the truck and took the turn far too quickly. For a moment, Alex thought they might careen off the edge of the highway and down the embankment. Into the lake. She didn't watch. She didn't gasp. Alex closed her eyes, feeling the centrifugal force thrust her aside, waiting for that moment the seat would drop away. The wheels screeched. Caleb sucked in a nervous breath. But Alex wanted to go over the edge. She yearned to feel weightless. She was not afraid. How could she fear anything after this? Fear implied that there was something to cherish, to savor in her life. She had abandoned her three-year-old daughter. If Sara was not already dead, then she would die soon. Hopefully, she was already gone. Hopefully, she walked into Kootenay Lake in a mindless delusion, not feeling the frigid water against her skin, not gasping for air, not flailing with useless strokes as the light of the sun drifted upwards, far out of reach, like an escaped helium balloon.   Hopefully. Because to Alex Maclean, that is how the world ends. Not with a struggle. Not with a scream. It ends without a sound. The sun drowned out by the crushing, blackening waters. Going, going.

RUDOLF KERKHOVEN

ABOUT THE AUTHOR

Rudolf Kerkhoven lives in the Vancouver area of British Columbia, Canada, with his wife and two children.

www.RudolfKerkhoven.com

@BownessBooks